No Home Training:

Say U Promise III

No Home Training:

Say U Promise III

Ms. Michel Moore

www.urbanbooks.net

Urban Books, LLC
97 N18th Street
Wyandanch, NY 11798

No Home Training: Say U Promise III

ISBN 13: 978-1-62286-779-0
ISBN 10: 1-62286-779-3

First Mass Market Printing September 2016
First Trade Paperback Printing April 2015
Printed in the United States of America

10 9 8 7 6 5 4 3 2 1

Distributed by Kensington Publishing Corp.
Submit orders to:
Customer Service
400 Hahn Road
Westminster, MD 21157-4627
Phone: 1-800-733-3000
Fax: 1-800-659-2436

Acknowledgments

Like many others before myself, I'd like to thank the Almighty Creator. At the times I was at my darkest hours, he offered me light. My mother Ella Fletcher has been a constant cheerleader of my talents when everyone else had seemingly abandoned my side. For her love, I'm forever grateful. My daughter, Tiffany aka author T.C. Littles is my true legacy that I leave the world. Although I have a deep attachment for each novel I've penned, hands down she's my greatest creation. My grandson Jayden is my second chance to 'get things right.' I want to especially acknowledge my husband John Moore for always providing unconditional devotion and the late night food runs you make, no questions asked.

My family and friends, Othello Lewis, Fleasha Curtis, Dwayne Fletcher, Yolanda McCormick, Jazmine Smith, Prince Campbell, Chris Tatum and Haji Sillah; I will forever be thankful for your support.

Acknowledgments

Lastly, my Urban Book family: Carl Weber, Natalie Weber, Denard "G" and my longtime homegirl in this book game Karen Mitchell-I appreciate y'all!

LOVE IS LOVE-MS. MICHEL MOORE

Chapter 1

Damn! I Almost Forgot!

The Question Is Did You?

While Kenya poured the coffee in the mugs, London looked in Chocolate Bunny's purse to turn off her cell phone that kept ringing. There she found a thick folded set of papers on the top and a few pictures. London read the first page of the legal documents, which was a purchase agreement, and couldn't believe her eyes. "I think you need to see this paper." She motioned to Kenya. "Now!"

"Oh, hell naw! What the fuck did we do?" Kenya yelled out with remorse after reading the paperwork. The papers were a deed to Chocolate Bunny's new house. They had her government name on them as well as another: Mr. Royce K. Curtis. The picture in her purse was an ultrasound that also had Royce's name on it. "All this time Royce's old-ass has been the one she's been fucking around with! Why didn't she just say that bullshit?"

Storm had awakened after getting a call from O.T. and had been at the door eavesdropping and cut her off. "Because after the big fight you and Royce had down at Alley Cats about me, we thought it'd be better for you not to know that Royce was our new connect. Plus it ain't really none of your business who Chocolate Bunny fucked with outside the club."

"Storm, I—" Kenya tried to explain.

"You know what, Kenya? From day one right off rip I should've known that you was gonna be trouble. My brother warned me, but I wouldn't listen. Now it's about to be a street war because you and your sidekick Paris fucked the fuck up! The streets of Dallas gonna run red! I'm done with your ass! You costing me too much!"

Kenya went into hysterics as she started throwing dishes against the wall and begging for Storm's forgiveness once again. She was crawling on her knees pleading with him not to leave her. London was now pissed as she watched her own flesh and blood lower herself by this pathetic display.

"Kenya! Get up off that damn floor! His ass ain't worth humiliating yourself like this!"

"Bitch! I 'bout done had enough of your instigating-ass too! Why don't you pack your bags and get to stepping!" Storm ran up in London's face. "Get your ass the fuck out my house!"

"This is my sister's house too!" London fired back.

"Well, Kenya, you gonna tell this bitch to be ghost or what?" Storm waited with a smirk on his face. "It's me or her, and I'm not playing around this time!" It grew quiet in the room as all eyes were on Kenya, who was breathing hard wiping the tears from her eyes. After a long pause she finally mumbled. "What did you say?" Storm demanded to hear.

"I said, 'London, would you mind getting a hotel room somewhere until me and Storm figure all of this mess out?'" Kenya, ashamed, failed to look at her twin sister. "Please it'll only be for a few days I promise!"

"Make that forever!" Storm shouted.

"Oh, it's like that?" London was heated. "I've put my life on hold for you and now you're taking his side over mine! How could you?"

"Please, London!" Kenya whimpered. "Please!"

Storm started to laugh and couldn't help himself as he taunted her. "You heard her, bitch! Go pack your shit and leave so I can get back to my life."

"Yeah, okay! Not at all a problem!" London headed up the stairs and to her room to gather her belongings. "You two deserve each other! I don't know how I stayed here in this madhouse this long anyhow!"

When she came back down Storm and Kenya were sitting on the couch talking. He was still dogging Kenya out, but stopped to sneer at London. "Don't worry. I already called your silly, jealous-ass a cab so you can go wait on the damn curb!"

Kenya was silent as London passed by and went into the kitchen to get something else before struggling to drag her bags to the front door. Just as she opened the front door the cab was pulling up and blew once. London looked back at her twin giving her one last chance. "You sure about this, Kenya? You're picking this slime ball dope dealer over me?"

Kenya lowered her head in embarrassment over her decision. After all they'd been through and stuck together the sisterly love and bond they shared was being torn apart.

"Okay, you know what it is, bitch! Now kick rocks!" Storm held the door open. "And don't bother us again! Kenya will call you so don't call her, you lonely ho!"

London was really overjoyed to leave. She'd had just about enough of Storm's disrespectful mouth, not to mention Kenya's spineless demeanor. With all her bags on the porch she spitefully turned around to face her sister and the man she'd so easily chosen over their bond. Vindictively London pulled up her T-shirt exposing a secret of her own that would shut a boisterous Storm up once and for all. Rubbing her slightly pudgy stomach in a circular motion looking down, London grinned, delivering the show-stopping revelation of the evening thus far. "It's all good. Don't worry about me and I ain't gonna be lonely for long, believe that!" London smirked as all eyes were on her. "Tell ya aunt Kenya and daddy Storm bye!"

"I don't understand! What the fuck are you talking about, London?" Kenya ran over to the door following her sister out to the cab. "What you mean daddy Storm? What is you talking about?"

Getting inside the cab London shut the door and rolled down the window. "Ask his ass what happened in the kitchen that night!" She pointed at the condo where Storm was standing face buried in his hands having a flashback. "He knows." London then instructed the cab to pull off leaving Kenya and Storm on the doorstep arguing. Smiling she opened one of her bags, which contained both guns and Chocolate Bunny's purse.

"Where to, miss lady?" the driver inquired.

"Yes, can you please take me to police head-quarters, the homicide division? I need to drop something off!"

And so the bullshit begins . . .

Chapter 2

New Thangs Poppin'

"You slept with my twin! You two-timing dirty-ass bastard! Tell me she's lying!" Kenya screamed, insane with fury, demanding answers. She stood knees buckling, teary-eyed on the front porch pounding her palm on the bricks of the condo watching London's cab disappear into the darkness of night. "Tell me that ain't ya baby she claims she carrying! Tell me! Tell me!" She lunged at her once seemingly faithful man who eased back barely missing the warranted attack. "Answer me, nigga!" The moonlight seemed to shine a direct spotlight on the couple as the reality of London's last cutthroat words took over the night. "You fucked her! You fucked my sister? In my damn house? This shit can't be happening! What she talking about, Storm? Tell me!"

Storm was left standing speechless. Mouth dry, head spinning, adrenalin racing, and heart pumping still trying to come to terms that he'd somehow mistakenly had sex with London, let alone gotten his fiancée's sister knocked up. He lowered his head in shame. "I . . . I . . ." Storm stumbled over his words attempting to offer some weak-ass explanation. "I must've been . . ."

"Must've been what, motherfucker?" Kenya, with contempt in her tone, drew back damn near to the sky smacking the dog shit outta Storm's face. "Or should I say sister fucker! How could you?" she pleaded with intense rage ready to swing on him again. "What about me? What about us?"

Before getting a chance to react to the confusing allegations or retaliate from the dooming sting of Kenya's strong hand, Storm was saved fortunately by his brother racing down the street swerving up into the driveway and jumping out his car.

"Hey, bro, can you believe what this one right here and Paris dumbasses done did?" O.T. broadcasted giving Kenya the sho'nuff evil eye. "They done messed our business all the way up! Royce ain't nothing more than an old coward, but even a mouse gotta roar when his girl and baby get done!"

"Whatever, Negro! It couldn't be helped!" Kenya yelled back while stepping inside the condo not in the mood for any more drama to entertain the neighbors. "Boy, bye! Go ya ass home for once and mind ya own business! It was an accident! I ain't have no choice! Now be ghost, we busy!"

"Busy?" O.T. brushed past Storm following his soon-to-be sister-in-law. "Is that what you retarded Detroit hoes call killing an innocent bitch and her baby and probably starting an all-out drug war? She ain't do nothing to y'all jealous tricks!"

Kenya paused turning around pointing her finger in O.T.'s face. "For one, if you would've been taking care of home instead of leaving all them unanswered questions floating around, Paris probably wouldn't have been tripping. And two, I was at the club shutting down like I was supposed to be doing. Your girl is the one who showed up with pajamas on waving a gun all around. Then she slipped up and let the next bitch gangster her for that motherfucker!" She was heated going into the kitchen to get the satchel off the table. "You can trust, if it weren't for me . . ."

Kenya's mouth shut as she quickly scanned the room searching for the brown paper bag containing Chocolate Bunny's purse and the two burners. Her eyes darted from the table to the floor, the floor to the counter, the counter to the stove, and back to the floor.

"If it weren't for you what?" O.T. was dead on her heels, standing tall, chest out, like he did no wrong waiting for a response.

"Awww hell naw! Ain't this about a bitch!"

"Awww hell naw what, Kenya?" Storm finally found the courage to speak up. "What's wrong?"

"Where's that bag?" She tossed a loaf of bread and a half-filled coffee mug onto the floor before kicking over two of the chairs, stooping down onto one knee so she could clearly see under the table. "I know I left it in here. I know I did, but I don't see nothing. No bag and no purse!"

"What bag?" O.T. questioned watching his older brother join in the frantic search. "What y'all looking for? And what fucking purse you talking 'bout? Y'all both done gone nuts in this crib!"

"I know London didn't! Please tell me she didn't!" An alarmed Kenya ignored O.T. placing her hand on her forehead, praying that her sister hadn't taken evidence to the murder.

"Baby, listen, I know you pissed," Storm hesitantly bargained, "but we gotta stop that cab she in and get them guns back. Ain't no telling what that crazy bitch gonna do next."

"Yeah, especially since ya nasty behind tossed her out to the streets! And was she a crazy bitch when you was hittin' it?"

"What!" O.T. yelled with his eyes bucked, leaning against the frame of the door. "You threw ol' girl out! And what guns in a bag y'all trying to get back? And damn! Who was hittin' it?"

"Ya scandalous brother, standing over there looking stupid, ran up in my sister behind my back and now she say she pregnant!"

"Damn, Kenya! You bullshittin'!"

"Naw, O.T. I wish I were, but I ain't!" Kenya ran toward the front door scrambling to grab her car keys. "Now I gotta find his no-good baby momma before she does some more trifling mess. The gun Paris had, not to mention the burner we kept behind the bar, is in that bag! This night just keeps getting better and better!"

"Y'all two stay here," O.T. insisted knowing his brother and Kenya had some serious talking to do. "I'll find her! It ain't but one way the cab could've gone. The main freeway is shut down and all the traffic is rerouted."

"Oh yeah, you right. I forgot about that," Storm blurted out not yet ready for the confrontation of a lifetime. "You sure you don't want me to bounce with you?"

"Did I hear you correct?" Kenya rolled her eyes in disbelief throwing her keys down onto the floor. "What'd you say?"

"I was just saying."

"You was just saying what?" She shifted her weight to one hip.

Storm shook his head shrugging his shoulders. "I was . . ."

"Nigga, please! You really tripping! Your best bet, right about now, is to get the fuck to explaining!"

"I don't even remember ever touching that girl! I can't stand the ho!" Storm started defending himself and getting his nuts back since O.T. was there watching him get chin checked by his girl.

"Yeah, dude, you's tripping, but hold it down, fam!" O.T. chuckled, amused, knowing his older sibling was about to catch it. "I got this, but on the real, you and her probably need to double back to Alley Cats, do some damage control and get rid of that body. Thelma and Louise messy dumbasses, nine outta ten, got my homegirl Chocolate Bunny stretched out on top of the bar like it ain't shit!"

"Fuck you with the all them jokes!" Kenya shouted as O.T. pulled out in search of London. "Fuck you!"

London

"Dang this traffic is backed up. Where is everybody going this late or should I say early?"

The cab driver glanced at the young antsy girl in his mirror and smiled. "Even at 4:05 in the morning ya gonna have slowdowns, Miss. With all the construction going on in town, what was once a twenty-minute ride has since doubled."

"Oh," London sighed, settling back in the seat, staring at the bright red glare coming from the broken brake lights of a rusty old Ford Tempo. "I guess what I need to do will just have to wait twenty extra minutes. I know the delay isn't your fault."

As she sat there with a suitcase on one side of the seat, clutching the brown paper bag, which held the fate of her sister and Paris, London closed her eyes trying her best to fight off the mildew smells of the car's interior that were making her increasingly nauseous.

"I'll hurry, Miss, but police headquarters is clear across town, so please bear with me."

"Okay," she mumbled, eyes still shut heart-breakingly reflecting on the ultrasound of Chocolate Bunny's innocent, now deceased, baby she had tucked in her own purse.

Every bump and pothole seemed to rattle the cab's frame shaking an already nervous London. As the car stopped and started, swerved and veered from lane to lane, she somehow managed to doze off. Before the expectant mother could get a chance to get into a deep sleep, she was abruptly awakened by the sound of the cab driver cursing.

"What in the hell is wrong with these folks?" he irately argued. "Why do some of our people think they above the law? Where are the police when you need them?"

"Huh?" London's ears got on high alert after hearing the word "police." "What's going on? What's wrong?"

"Some out-of-control lunatic behind us is dodging in and out of traffic!" the driver hissed watching defensively out his rear mirror. "He's gonna cause an accident if he ain't careful!"

London gazed out the back window just in time to see a pair of high-beam headlights loom past, barely avoiding sideswiping the cab. As she twisted her body back around to the front, the bag she was holding fell to the floor causing the two guns to fall out. "Oh no!" She panicked leaning over to conceal them.

"Hey what you doing?" the driver yelled out to the mystery driver. "What do you want?"

When London raised her head, she was greeted by the unpleasant sight of O.T.'s huge closed fist banging on the window.

"Open the door, London!"

"Mister, are you crazy?" the driver answered for her.

"Open the damn door, girl!" This time O.T. used his Tims to put a massive size-twelve dent in the door.

"Leave me alone! Leave me alone!"

"Do you know this man?" the driver questioned London, scared his window was about to be shattered in pieces. "Why is he doing this to my cab?"

"London, I'm not playing with ya ass! Open this motherfucker!" O.T. ordered pulling on the door handle as other drivers looked on.

Traffic let up slightly and temporary the cabby was able to escape the attack on his vehicle, moving up three or four yards before stopping again. O.T., forced to run alongside the car, was now even more agitated and determined for London to get out.

"Should I call the police, Miss? I don't want trouble!"

"No, no, just wait!" London was confused on what to do next. "Let me just crack the window and see what he wants."

"No! If you want to argue with your boy-friend, take your belongings and get out the cab! Please!"

Bam. Bam. Bam.

"I'm done with the games!" O.T. promised with certaintly in his voice. "Now get out this fucking cab and let's go home!"

"Leave me alone!" London begged trying to press her body over to the other side of the seat her suitcase was occupying.

The driver knew that his cab would surely have more damage he would've doubtlessly been responsible for paying if he continued to let what he believed to be a late-night/early morning lovers' quarrel to go on. He then made the cowardly decision to unlock the rear door giving O.T. full and complete access to his now distraught passenger. Hearing the clicking sound and the quick motion of the cab's door being flung open, London got chills not know-ing what to expect next.

"Hurry up before this traffic starts to move or some of these nosey suckers call the damn cops!"

"Get your hands off me!" London screamed as she was being manhandled across the cracked imitation leather seats.

"Or what?"

"Don't touch me!" She tried squirming away.

"Come on with the dumb shit, Miss Lady!"

"Who do you think you are? Leave me alone!"

"Shut the fuck up with all the dramatics and let's go!"

O.T. reached over retrieving the suitcase with one hand as he made London step out onto the curb with the other forcefully marching her to his car.

"Okay! Okay! Just stop yanking on my arm! You're hurting me!"

"Well come on!" O.T. loosened his grip tossing he luggage in his vehicle's back seat. "Where's he bag?"

"What?" London tried in vain to hide the worn, ripped sack behind her back. "What are you talking about?"

"Cut the act, girl, you better than that. If I'm out here, snatching ya black-ass out this damn cab, you know I already know! So just give me the mystery bag with them burners, climb ya silly pregnant-ass in the car, and let's ride!"

"Where are we going?" London looked straight ahead out the windshield, arms folded, embarrassed O.T. knew the whole awful truth. "Because I'm not going back to Kenya's!"

"Don't worry. I don't think ya ass wanted back over there anyhow. And besides all that, where was you on your way to with these guns anyway?"

"Nowhere!" London sadly realized she really could've turned her own flesh and blood in to the authorities. "I don't have anybody else here in town I even know."

O.T. started the car and drove off dipping onto a dimly lit side street several blocks over, and parked. Turning off the headlights he instinctively ducked down as the red and blue flashing lights of a police squad car flew past in the direction they'd just left. Carefully easing in an upright position O.T. grabbed the burners as he stepped out. Hitting the button release popping the trunk, the seasoned lawbreaker cleverly hid the guns in a small corner section that he had designed for such an occasion. The stash box, which was under a few old oil-stained football jerseys, covered by two spare tires, jumper cables, and a rusty jack, was ideal.

Making sure no one in their right mind would want to touch or disturb anything in the trunk he pissed across the entire contents. Even though the smell would start to reek when the trunk got heated it was the lesser of two evils. Smelly trunk or catching several cases! You do the math! Fuck the cops! And fuck them finding two guns he knew for sure had more than a couple of bodies on them; he'd scrub his shit out later! For now it was time to ride!

Hopping back inside, he stared at London who was crying hysterically coming to terms that her once perfect life was now shot to hell.

"All you females going nuts tonight! It must be a full moon!" O.T. rubbed his chin taking his cell phone off his hip. "Let me at least tell Storm and Kenya I got them thangs back. Then I'll figure out something."

"All right." London sobbed into her shirtsleeve as she watched him make the call. "Thank you."

Meanwhile, Back at the Condo . . .

Kenya slammed the front door almost off the hinges before turning around eagerly to resume her tirade and once again get off into Storm's ass. "Now back to you!"

"Please, sweetie! Just listen!" He clutched his hands together wishing all of this was just an awful nightmare and he would soon wake up to a home-cooked breakfast in bed. "I swear to God I don't know what happened!"

"How can you honestly stand here and take a damn cop to the bullshit? Either you fucking nuts or you think I am!" Kenya insisted. "Whatever the case my sister is pregnant! Now is you the father or what?"

"Okay, okay, okay." Storm attempted taking her hand to lead her to the couch. "Can we talk quietly?"

"You mean as quiet as you and London was when y'all was banging right beneath my nose? You mean that quiet?"

"Please, baby!"

"Don't call me baby ever again! You can save that title for your unborn child. Now tell me what in the hell exactly happened and when! And you better tell the truth or I swear!"

Storm sat down and tried to relive that disastrous night months ago. He now knew why London had done a 360 when it came to the way she looked at him or the way she'd speak to him when they were alone. It all made painful sense. She, not Kenya, was the first one to get a taste of his hard pipe the night he discovered he could get an erection again. He remembered being hung over the next day with a headache pounding hard enough to knock the average man on his knees. That was the day too, the once self-made kingpin, came to the realization he'd had enough of feeling sorry for himself and others pitying him.

The cards were dealt so he distinctively played his hand the best he was raised to. Now, bingo! Just like that, in a snap of the fingers, at a drop of a dime, he was back where he started from, fucked in the game. London was again the ultimate cause of his life to be in utter turmoil.

"Okay, baby. I mean, Kenya," he caught himself. "All I can recall was that night I had gotten real drunk. You were gone to the club and London was here. I do think I remember that much."

"And, don't stop," Kenya demanded, taking a seat across from Storm, rolling her eyes. "Then what?"

"I was thinking about you all that day. I was hoping that you wouldn't get tired of me and the fact that I wasn't hitting you off in the sex department like I used to."

"Humph." Twisting her neck, sucking her teeth with ghettoness expertise that would put most gutter rats to shame, Kenya urged him to continue. "Where is this going?"

"You know back then I was drinking heavy and popping them painkillers like a motherfucker."

"So!"

"So all them chemicals in a nigga's body seriously fucks with his brain and shit! Plus, damn, I thought my leg wasn't gonna never be right." Storm got on the defensive as he tried to momentarily flip the script. "That stuff had me bugging most of the time and acting a straight fool! I was half out my mind most the damn day and all the nights back then!"

"And what exactly that got to do with having sex with my sister?" Kenya stood to her feet passionately pacing the room tired of the back-and-forth word game she and he were playing. "In a hot minute I'm about to go psycho on your ass if you don't just tell the truth."

"I'm trying, but remember, Kenya, the truth don't come so easy in this house!"

"Nigga, please don't bring that way back when shit up! You better try harder!" Kenya threatened picking up a small but heavy marble statue. "I'm done playing!"

"Damn! I am. Just go easy!" Storm reasoned. "The whole incident is cloudy in my mind. Somehow I must've mistaken her for you and let her seduce me or something."

"She seduced you? London? My sister?"

"Yeah, you should hear some of the slick shit she be kicking when you ain't around. If I really raped her, why she ain't call the damn police? Shit, we all just finished eating dinner earlier! I'm telling you, Kenya, ya sister been on a mission."

"Well it seems like mission accomplished around this bitch! And why this the first time I done heard about her supposedly chasing behind you?"

"I love ya, girl! I'd never do anything to hurt you." Storm eased his way over to his fiancée trying his best to embrace her. "I love you."

"Oh, hell naw! Get your hands off me!" She was strong, not shedding one single solitary tear even though she felt like her inner soul was ripped out her body. Her fatigued frame trembled as she remained firm. "Don't touch me!"

Storm dropped to his knees pleading with her for forgiveness. Not too proud to beg or cry he started back on the blame game. "Listen, babe!" He wrapped his arms around her waist while trying to press his head against her stomach. "I'd never do anything intentionally to hurt you. You my world! Your sister is making all these allegations about me and I don't even really remember shit! Matter of fact, how you know it's even true? She probably was lying just to get back at you for having my back."

Kenya's arms dropped down at her side and she released the statue letting it hit the carpet. As she let her fingertips rub the sides of her blue jeans feeling every fiber, she closed her eyes praying that he was right. "What am I supposed to believe?"

"Well think about it." Storm looked up toward Kenya's eyes. "If London really is knocked up, you know nine outta ten it's my brother's baby. You already know how they do what they do!"

"I guess." Kenya started to move her hands and slowly wiped the tears from his face. "I just don't know why she would do something like that. My sister ain't even cut like that."

Storm, relieved he'd temporarily dodged the bullet persuading Kenya to calm down, got onto his feet kicking the statue, and would-be weapon, to the side on the sly. Holding her face close to his he kissed her on the forehead. "Listen up. I know this ain't over and I swear we gonna get to the bottom of her lies, but for real, for real, we need to go down to the club and see what's what, ya feel me?"

"But—" Kenya hesitated not yet ready to let the heart- wrenching subject go so easily.

"But nothing." Storm reached over grabbing Kenya's car keys off the floor and headed to the door. "Your sister done lied on me and started all this madness. It's because of her my leg is fucked up and my ear is deformed! She ain't doing shit but trying to drive a wedge between us. Now we've been through too much to let anybody do that shit! So come on, baby, let's get down to Alley Cats before it's too late! I'll drive!"

"Yeah, okay," Kenya finally agreed knowing Storm would make the Chocolate Bunny situation go away. After all she'd committed murder. Even if it was to save Paris's life, nevertheless it'd be considered coldblooded murder of that skank and her baby.

Chapter 3

Truth Be Told

Controversy

"What up, my dude?"

"Shit, on our way down to the club. Did you handle that for me or what?"

"Yeah." O.T. glanced over at London who was still a mess. "I got them in the stash and ol' girl sitting right next to me."

"That lying bitch!" Storm blurted out trying to further defend himself in front of Kenya. "Fuck her!"

Kenya was still heated at her twin, but sick and tired of Storm and O.T. dogging her sister out. After all, Storm was right and had made a good point. She could've been just lying to get back at her. And considering all the drama she'd brought into London's once simple barely complicated life she did have it coming. "Y'all can stop speaking about her like that!"

"She ain't nothing but a troublemaker. Now I see why you kept the tramp a secret!"

"Listen, Storm! That's my blood!"

"Yeah, she the same blood who was about to turn you in to the rat-ass police," he condescendingly lectured.

"What the fuck ever!"

O.T. had enough of hearing the two of them argue. "Hey, hey! Y'all can do all that nonsense later. Where y'all want me to take ol' girl? I got moves to make myself."

"She ain't welcome or wanted back at my crib!" Storm harshly proclaimed as he drove.

Kenya took a deep breath and angrily snatched the cell phone out Storm's hand. "Let me talk to my damn sister!"

After a brief second and urging from O.T., London stubbornly got on the line. "Hello."

"London," Kenya hissed. "Why you take those guns out my house? What was you gonna do with them?"

"I don't know." London puzzled. "I just—"

"And not only that. Why'd you lie on my man? You know y'all didn't have sex! He don't want you!"

"What! Is that what he told you?" London screamed making O.T. take notice. "Well he's partially right, we didn't have sex! He raped me!"

"He raped you!" Kenya shrieked in disbelief at her twin's outlandish claim.

"My brother did what?" O.T.'s reaction was instant shock. "Come the fuck on!"

"Yeah, that's right. Your precious man is nothing more than a cheating animal on the prowl. He held me down and raped me on your kitchen floor in front of the refrigerator!" London informed her sister as well as O.T. who was for once quiet. "I didn't want to do it! He made me!"

"Let me get this straight!" Kenya seethed with burning hatred as her stomach started to churn and her hands shivered. "You saying Storm forced his self on you? Is that right? Just like you claimed your college professor did?"

London was getting fed up. She was truly innocent having had just about enough of all the insults, attacks on her character, and now dragging things up from her past. "Not that the two incidents have anything in common maybe except the fact that both the guys are slime balls, your man assaulted me! On Gran's grave I promise!"

"Well he said he ain't touched you! Let alone take the pussy!"

"And you believe him?"

"Well, he said that."

"Stop taking up for him, Kenya!" London begged wiping her face with an old piece of balled-up tissue out her purse. "He got you wrapped around his little finger!"

"He said he ain't touch you!" Kenya unconfidently repeated as she watched a nervous Storm grip up on the steering wheel as small beads of sweat started to form on his forehead.

"Stop saying that lie! I'm telling you what happened! He grabbed me from the back and knocked me down on the floor! I even scratched him across his neck trying to get him off me!" The aggravated twin ranted with rage. "But since you so busy defending his no-good butt, we'll just wait and see what happens in a few months then that'll convince you who's telling the truth."

"Stop lying, London! Why you doing this?"

"I know you weren't trying to major in anything but boys when you were in school and, Kenya, I've always known you aren't the smartest apple in the bunch, but you can trust one thing for sure, DNA don't lie!"

"Naw! It ain't true!" Kenya trapped in denial finally let go all her tears. "You lying just trying to break us up! You lying, London! You lying! You just jealous 'cause I got a man and you don't! You always wanted to be me!"

"Here's a few words of advice my naive two-faced twin sister, instead of worrying about me and my baby breaking you two up, you need to be concerned with the judge breaking y'all criminals up when they arrest you for murder and him for all that drug dealing."

With that exchange, a frustrated London folded her arms after handing the phone to O.T. who took it back, shutting it slowly, never saying a word as he drove off.

Bottom Line Is . . .

"How did you get that scratch on your neck?" Kenya turned her full attention back to interrogate Storm who now knew he was busted.

"What scratch? Don't let her get in your head!" He tried downplaying the million dollar question. "I don't know what you or her talking 'bout!"

"That one!" She pointed, deliberately digging her nails deep into his skin as she twisted his neck to reveal the obvious.

"That shit hurt!" He snatched back trying to keep his eyes focused on the narrow road. "You bugging!"

"Naw, you is! You did fuck her!" Kenya balled up her fist socking Storm hard as she could in the side of his neck causing the car to cross the lines into the next lane.

Pulling over to the side then slamming on the brakes he charged over at Kenya smashing her face against the passenger window. With his palm painfully pressing her cheek, his fingers tangled up in her hair. Holding his woman there as she helplessly gasped for air struggling to break free, Storm laid his law down. Kenya could feel his angry lips touch her ear as he spoke.

"I don't know what the hell happened that night with your damn sister, but I do know I'm a fucking grown-ass man and you ain't about to just keep putting your hands on me disrespecting a nigga like I'm not! So sit back, shut the fuck up, and know your role!" he hissed as his breath grew hotter. "Let me handle this situation at the club you and Paris created! Then we can deal with whatever! You understand?"

Kenya bossed up and determinedly refused to respond as the window her face was crushed against started to fog up and get misty.

"Did you hear me!" Storm demandingly applied more pressure while waiting for her answer. "I know you hear me talking to you! Don't you?"

"Yeah," she finally muttered in a whisper, barely loud enough for him to make out. "I heard you."

"Good, then chill!"

When Storm released her, Kenya opted for the time being to do just that, chill. Moving her matted hair out her tear-filled face, attempting to catch her breath, the exhausted female folded her arms furious, still full of questions with no answers seemingly in sight.

New Roommates . . .

O.T. took London to a hotel that was all too familiar to her. It was the same place Kenya and she stayed when she first arrived in Dallas. After the incompatible, quiet couple checked in getting the plastic credit card—like room key from the front desk, they headed to the elevator. O.T. carried London's bags as he looked down toward her stomach wondering if his niece or nephew was actually growing inside of her.

"What's wrong with you?"

"Nothing," he replied stepping onto the elevator pushing the eighth-floor button. "Just thinking."

"Oh, yeah." London smirked with a sarcastic attitude. "I bet you were."

When they reached the room, O.T. put the bags on the floor and slid the key in the sensor. No sooner than the light flashed green London reached over pushing the door open. Coming all the way in the navy blue and ivory white decorated suite, the pair stood silently staring at one another.

"Well." O.T. was the first to speak. "Is it true or not?"

"Is what true?"

"Is you gonna have Storm's kid?"

"I'm pregnant. So yeah, it is true."

"So y'all was fucking behind ya sister's back huh? You's straight-up grimy for that one, baby girl! But then again, a guy knows firsthand ya got that freaky bone in ya!"

"Naw, it wasn't like that!" London vehemently protested walking to the window turning her back shamefully on O.T. "Storm raped me! How many times do I have to say it?"

"Come on now, girl! My brother ain't never ever had to take the pussy from no bitch! Chicks be throwing the cat on him left and right, day after day!" he viciously argued raising his voice. "So why would he strong-arm ya silly, hot-ass?"

"You should be asking him why he did what he did, not giving me the third degree! And don't call me a hot-ass!" she yelled shoving him out her way running to the bathroom to throw up. "Go say that to your beloved Paris."

"Whatever, tramp! Getting some of my bro-ther's dick must've given you back your little confidence!" He flashed back to the afternoon she deep throated his manhood as he posted up in the doorway watching her down on her knees at the white porcelain toilet. "Don't forget, a nigga like me know better!"

"Fuck all you dirty, immoral crooks!" London directed as she wiped the corners of her mouth. "I'm going back home to Detroit!"

"Like I really give a shit! I was just giving your stank-ass a piece of conversation!" Busting out laughing, O.T. took his cell off his hip making a call to check on one of his dope spots. "I'm just glad I had the fucking sense to make you swallow my seed!" He choked up on his dick and nuts. "'Cause you on the ziggy nut boom around these parts!"

"How can you continue to be so mean and heartless day after day?" London got on her feet. "Didn't your parents teach you or your brother any manners?"

"Sorry me and him weren't like y'all. We wasn't born with no silver spoons in our mouth, so fuck you!"

Chapter 4

It's On Now!

Done Is Done

"Shit! It's too late!" Storm hit the headlights so they could be incognito. "These dudes already here!"

A huge flatbed with flashing lights and several cars that Storm immediately recognized as some of Royce's soldiers surrounded Chocolate Bunny's car. With their cell phones in hand, Storm and Kenya could only assume the guys were conversing with their boss, informing him that his woman was nowhere to be found. As the couple hid near the dark edge of Alley Cats' parking lot where Kenya sat nervously regretting her earlier actions now realizing that she was in a world of trouble, her eye involuntary twitched.

"You think they know?"

"Hell naw!" Storm turned to face his woman. "You best believe if they found ol' girl it would've been more motherfuckers out here including the goddamn police!"

"I guess you right."

"I know I am!" Storm confidently replied. Watching the group circle Chocolate Bunny's automobile as the tow truck driver attached the chains to hook up, Storm grew annoyed trying to figure out his next move. "What in the hell did you do to her whip?"

"I ain't do nothing." Kenya spoke softly like someone other than her and Storm was inside the car. "That shit was on flat when the bitch finished her shift. Her and the rest of the girls came out and they was like that."

"Somebody had to do something. Ain't nobody just gonna catch four flats at one time."

"I said I didn't, so stop blaming me for the crap!" Kenya fumed getting louder when it dawned on her that not only had Paris involved her in murder; she'd obviously set the whole thing up by letting the air out the tires or slicing them.

Beep, beep, beep. The truck backed up, lights flaring and roared out the front of the lot, with Royce's boys following close behind on alert as if they were serving as personal body guards or pallbearers to Chocolate Bunny's fallen car.

"Okay, it's all good. I think they gone." Storm threw the car in drive and cautiously crept to the rear entrance of the club near the Dumpsters where Kenya directed him to park. Glancing down at the car's digital clock before getting out, and looking up to the moon, which was rapidly disappearing, he schemed, realizing the time factor was crucial. "We should be able to fix this bullshit before the sun comes all the way up."

"I hope so." A tormented Kenya looked around for any signs of movement, putting one sneaker on the ground keeping the other in the car.

"Damn! Come on!" Storm motioned searching deep behind the second to the left black and gray huge metal containers that were serving as somewhat of a makeshift tomb. "I'm gonna need your help."

Forgetting that less than thirty or so minutes ago they were at each other's throats, Kenya and Storm were now once again functioning as a team. Several strong yanks and a few tugs on the extra thick body, he soon thankfully unwedged the stiffening corpse. He couldn't help but feel a little bit of sympathy for Royce who not only was gonna suffer the loss of his girl, but his unborn child.

Furious that he was forced to dispose of a chick whose only true crime was shaking her ass to get that loot he shouted out orders in the empty parking lot to Kenya. "Do you at least got the alarm off and the door open yet?"

"Yeah," Kenya did a quick search "I spy" peeking around the deserted building. "It's open."

"Well come get her feet!" he demanded as he tried unsuccessfully to drag his suddenly deceased employee without ripping a gaping hole in the back of her head causing anymore incriminating evidence to spill into the concrete pavement. "This bitch heavy as shit! I can see stomping Nicole out, but damn ya had to kill her?"

"I told you I ain't have no choice. She had Paris's gun about to pull the trigger!" Kenya shut her eyes walking backward with her victim's ankles clutched in her hands.

After winning the battle of getting the body into the club, Storm tossed her onto the middle of the kitchen floor along with her scuffed sandals that had fallen off. Bam! The murdered dancer landed face first probably breaking a few bones that she didn't feel anyway. Storm then reached over hitting the light switch for the kitchen. Pushing her over on her back revealing the true ghastly sight of Chocolate Bunny live and in motherfucking color, he shook his head with disgust.

Her T-shirt and miniskirt were ripped from all the dragging to and from the Dumpster and more than a couple of tracks from her $400 weave were hanging loose. With the apparent bloody wounds from the gunshots soaking her grimy clothes and the foul-smelling thick caked burgundy dried remains of her miscarried fetus in between her legs splattered on both thighs, she was center stage on display at Alley Cats one last time.

The usual hard core drug dealer closed his eyes briefly for a moment of silence out of respect for a female he'd stuck his dick in once or twice back in the day, then grabbed Chef Terry's always sharpened meat cleaver that was hanging on the kitchen's overhead rack and went to work. Keeping his mind preoccupied with the haunting memory of abuse he suffered at the hands of his stepfather he murdered as a youth, Storm's heart went numb.

Kenya's empty stomach bubbled in pain as she instinctively turned her face away trying to focus on the stainless steel walk-in refrigerator and the industrial-sized oven, hoping when she turned back in the other direction her victim would've somehow magically disappeared. But hell naw! No dice! Unfortunately no matter how hard the ex-stripper and drug mule turned business woman now murderer concentrated and prayed, she couldn't block out the haunting sounds of her man Storm who'd initiated his plan of disposing of "the problem" by hacking, cutting, slashing, and mangling skin, followed by twisting, ripping, and breaking bones that were on the very verge of rigor mortis.

With every limb that he mutilated the fatal gunshot sound seemed to echo repeatedly in Kenya's mind. Consumed with culpability for her drastic now regrettable actions she covered her ears with both hands, yet still couldn't drown out her guilt. The wrist, one leg, then the next, a snap severing the elbow and a clean crack of the neck all seemed not to bother Storm, who had it embedded in his brain that he was running interference, saving Kenya from a definite prison bid.

In about a solid hour the heinous deed was done and the body parts including Chocolate Bunny's undisturbed upper torso was stuffed into a huge oversized duffle bag and thrown into the trunk. Disinfecting the small work area he used for his ghetto version autopsy he then washed his hands with hot scalding water. After the weary couple snatched the security surveillance tapes out the recorder and reset the alarm system they drove off, merging in with the early morning rush-hour traffic.

"Instead of driving all the way out to the crib, I'm gonna drop you off at Paris's then get rid of that situation." He signaled to the rear of the car. "You can clue that ho in and make sure she keeps her damn mouth shut."

"Okay," Kenya eagerly agreed not overly anxious to ride with a chopped-up dead body. "I got some stuff to tell her anyhow." She raised her eyebrow letting Storm know that she wasn't done with the whole London and him thing.

Royce

"I wonder where in the hell she's at." Royce's long fingers slowly combed through his salt-and-pepper coarse beard as his seasoned voice tried hard to show no signs of worry and downplay his concern. "She must've caught a ride with one of her little dancer friends or something."

"Yeah, boss, ya probably right." With his thick sandy-colored dreads swinging in the brisk night air, Marco chirped back pacifying his boss's words as he and the fellas stood around in disgust aggravated by being ordered away from a high-stakes dice game on a dry run chasing a ho. "It's deserted in the lot and the club is dark as a motherfucker! Ya girl probably got tired of waiting and just dipped."

"Well, you cats just go ahead and have the car towed to the mechanic's shop and I'll get new tires thrown on it in the morning," Royce grumbled rushing to get off the line so he could once again for the hundredth time try to call his baby-momma-to-be. "Later."

"All right, peace!" Marco, Royce's young headstrong lieutenant, placed his cell back on the side of his rhinestone-studded belt laughing with the guys about their "past his prime" boss tripping on Chocolate Bunny going A.W.O.L. If they knew her like half the niggas in the city knew her, Nicole Daniels's black nasty behind was most likely somewhere across town, laid up with the next dude's dick stuffed in her mouth.

Hell, less than two weeks before Royce made the asshole decision to make the off-the-hook sack chaser his official wifey; she did a private party for Marco and a crew of motherfuckers out the projects. Needless to say, the go-getter bitch had no worldly limits to what she did to get her hustle on that hot summer night. Now, just like that, Royce expected an ambitious power-seeking Marco and the rest of the team to respect that good tricking stank whore as their crew's first lady, just because she was pregnant with his old seed. Shitttttt! They all questioned his leadership.

Enough Already . . .

Dang, what's taking her ass so long to come to the door? Kenya grew inpatient reaching in her pocket for her keys that also had Paris's spare set on the ring. *She probably asleep! Where I should be, if it weren't for her!*

An eerie feeling came over her as she crossed the threshold of the silent apartment, but she passed it off as jitters after what she'd just witnessed Storm do. Paris's favorite scent of jasmine filled the air and everything seemed completely normal until Kenya looked into the living room, which was unusually cluttered with magazines, half-eaten bags of chips, balled-up candy wrappers, and old love novels. The pillows on the sofa weren't perfect as Paris would always keep them and a substantial layer of dust was easily viewable on the end tables.

What the fuck? Kenya was bewildered as she passed the kitchen noticing the sink was overflowing with dirty dishes. As she neared the bedroom she called out to Paris once, then twice, getting no answer either time. Going over to her friend's closet, Kenya took one of Paris's track suits off the hanger and changed her clothes. Messy from the night's events, she looked in the mirror and shuddered at the dark bags that were forming under her eyes. *Where this crazy girl at now? I thought I told her to stay in the house! Her unpredictable-ass probably out ruining the next chick's life! Making her look as bad as I do!*

Knowing that Storm left her stranded for the time being as he shot a move, she decided to make herself useful and at least bust the suds until Paris came home. Maybe it would calm her nerves; plus, she knew as exhausted as she was, if she even sat down on the couch, she'd be out for the count, more than likely missing Storm's call to pick her back up.

Heading into the kitchen she started sorting out the dishes and turned on the hot water. After a few seconds of searching for the dish soap, Kenya walked back down the hallway pushing the bathroom door, which was cracked with the light out, all the way open.

"Oh shit! Naw, Paris! Naw!" Wide-eyed with shock Kenya discovered her best friend sprawled out on the marble floor with a busted lip and several bottles of opened pills nearby. "What in the fuck did you do? What did you do? Damn!" Bending down grabbing both hands shaking Paris's arms in an attempt to get her up, a hysterical Kenya screamed. "Wake up! Wake up!"

Getting no results, she scrambled to her feet bolting to the front room frantically searching the unkempt apartment for the phone. Dialing 911 while rushing back to the bathroom, Kenya wet a washcloth with cold water, wiping Paris's face, which confusingly had a black and blue swollen bottom lip.

"Nine-one-one, what's the emergency?"

"Yes, I think my friend has overdosed!"

"Is your friend conscious or alert?"

"No!"

"What type of chemical is involved?"

"I don't know! Just some pills! Please send help!" Kenya pleaded.

"Miss, the computer shows that you're at 19348 North Street? Is that correct?"

"Yes! Shady Tree Estates, apartment fifty-eight on the north side!"

"Okay, stay on the line. Paramedics are being dispatched."

"Please hurry!"

The operator listened to Kenya scream and cry. "Miss, calm down. A rig has responded and is already en route to your location. Is your friend a male or a female?"

"A female."

"Does she have a pulse?"

"Yes, but hurry up! Please!"

"Can you read what the bottle says on the label?"

"What difference does it make? Just send help!"

Tossing the cordless phone down Kenya rocked an unresponsive Paris in her arms talking to her until she heard the piercing high-pitched sirens of the ambulance. Twenty long, grueling minutes later, Kenya found herself in a crowded hospital waiting room placing a call to O.T., Storm, and Paris's older cousin, Tangy, who had just gotten out of jail. Thirty short minutes after that, all-out hell broke loose.

"What happened to my cuz?" The questions came one after another as soon as Tangy bolted through the doors.

"Tangy, girl, I came over to the apartment and found her in the bathroom passed out cold!"

"From what? Why?"

Kenya anticipated when she informed her, the real deal, she would trip, but at this point there wasn't any reason for keeping secrets. The doctor would come from the back sooner or later and say what Paris had done anyhow: tried to commit suicide.

"She had taken a lot of pills."

"What!" Tangy snatched her baseball cap off showing her freshly braided, thick, perfectly lined cornrows. With saggy, oversized blue jeans dragging the hospital floor, barely allowing her small Tims to be seen, the flat-chested dyke pounded her fist inside her hand. "Why would she do some dumb shit like that?"

"I don't know, girl," Kenya lied opting not to throw O.T. under the train, considering he was innocent of what she and Paris had been accusing him of for months. "She was under a lot of stress I guess."

Tangy's wifey, Vanessa, who used to dance at Alley Cats, was by her side rubbing her back in hopes of calming her down. She was a former headliner act, Cash-N-Go, a true freak about her business who went both ways. Kenya never trusted her around Storm and Storm never trusted her around Kenya. Vanessa was a temptress. Now she was Tangy's main chick and was known by reputation to cut any ho's throat who came near her. She didn't care if Kenya was once her boss or not, Tangy was hers! Period!

"Where in the hell was O.T.? And matter of fact where in the fuck is he at now?"

"Tangy, relax," Kenya urged, patting her shoulder trying to ease any impending tension and reassure her. "I called him and he's on his way."

"Yeah, when he get out the next bitch's pussy, with his scurvy self! Everybody knows that nigga a player!"

"Hey, baby, let's go over here and wait." Insecure with the next female consoling her woman, Vanessa tugged at Tangy's tatted-up arm. "I'll get you a soda until we hear something."

Before that could happen, O.T. causally strolled through the emergency sliding doors with no great urgency as he chopped it up on his cell phone. Tangy broke away from her girl and recklessly flew up into O.T.'s face as if she had wings.

"Nigga, where in the fuck was you when my cousin needed you?"

"Bitch! If you don't get ya little steaming hot dragon breath out my face I'm gonna beat the brakes off you! Ya heard me!" His face frowned up that someone, a female no less, was jumping bad with him. "Don't you see a pimp is busy?"

"I ain't scared of ya pathetic-ass!" Tangy continued to rant pressing her luck as her arms waved wildly causing a scene. "You ain't gonna do shit to me!"

"You can strap a plastic dick on all ya want, but, Tangy, you ain't no dude! So get ya 'once a month bleeding wish the fuck ya could piss standing up' ass the hell away from me before I forget you's a bitch!" O.T. didn't move one inch or even end the call he was on.

"Or what?" Tangy boldly challenged getting closer in his face as the people sitting down looked on. "What ya gonna do?"

"Listen, carpet muncher! Ya better go on over there and kick it with ya girl before I stick my dick up in her again!" He blew Vanessa a kiss.

"What!" Tangy swole up looking at O.T. then Vanessa then back to O.T. "What the fuck you talkin' 'bout?"

"Listen, baby." Vanessa tried explaining. "I—"

"Oh, you didn't know? Don't get it twisted!" O.T. taunted, cell phone still pressed to his ear. "I hit that about a month ago when you was locked up and thanks to ya non fucking with a dildo-ass the pussy was tight as a son of a bitch! So every time you eating that cat, you's really sucking my dick!" O.T. jerked at his pants. "I had ya girl calling my name all night long! Ain't that right, Vanessa?"

"Please, y'all!" Kenya tried mediating. "Leave it alone, O.T. We all here for Paris remember?"

"Naw, sis, naw. Tangy wanna be a man so bad," he ridiculed. "So let her man up and deal with the fact her old lady was calling me daddy, begging me to tear that thang up!"

Tangy instantly got caught in her feelings and sucker-punched O.T. in face. He laughed at the lightweight hit, but responded quickly. Just as

Kenya predicted: absolute undeniable chaos. Fuck the security guards who weren't anywhere to be found no way. Having had enough, not holding back one bit, towering over her, O.T. angrily blew Tangy's mouth out with ease just like he'd done her cousin's a few hours earlier. Temporarily losing her balance, falling onto one of the vending machines, she shook the punch off taking it like a true champ. Tyson and Ali would've been proud!

Petrified knowing full well she was in the wrong, Vanessa rushed over to intervene on the potentially dangerous confrontation before her hot-tempered, relentless five foot three gladiator woman really got her ass kicked and she had to slice O.T. up to prove her love.

"Please, Tangy! Leave it alone!"

"Yeah, like I was saying," O.T. resumed his phone conversation not missing a beat, "I'll check it out for you."

When he finally ended his call, he pulled Kenya over to the side near the water fountain finding out exactly what over-the-top dramatically designed stunt his attention-starved now ex-girlfriend Paris had done this time. Shift change had just taken place when the weary doctor emerged from behind the closed doors with an update on Paris's condition.

"It was touch and go for a while, but we have her stabilized. She'll be moved to the ICU then probably to the mental observation ward."

"Doctor, can I see her?" Tangy spoke nursing a fresh semi-swollen lip. "I'm her cousin."

"Yes, but only for a few minutes." The doctor subsequently looked toward O.T. "Excuse me, are you her husband? She kept calling out for you."

"Naw, Doc, I ain't the one. I'm just a dude the dumb chick used to know." O.T. callously headed for the door now knowing Paris would live. "Come on, Kenya, I done wasted enough time! Let's roll! Storm wants me to drop you by the crib."

"I always hated my little cousin being with your dirty behind!" Tangy angrily said wanting to still fight.

"Bitch! Get the hell on before I bend you over and give you some of this good dick too."

"You ain't shit!" Tangy shouted back. "And it ain't over!"

"Men ain't about nothing!" Vanessa cosigned with her girl knowing they would beef later about O.T.'s claim.

Kenya wanted to stay and see Paris, but the harsh realism was Storm obviously had played Houdini with Chocolate Bunny and now she could deal with the predicament between him and her sister. Before leaving the hospital, Kenya made Tangy promise to call her later with an update. Much to a jealous Vanessa's disliking, she stood back as the two females embraced comforting the other.

Daybreak had already come when Kenya got home. Finding Storm stretched out on the couch snoring, also drained herself, she decided to let it go for the time being. Standing in the doorway wanting to get a glass of orange juice before going to bed, she couldn't seem to bring herself to go into the kitchen, let alone open the refrigerator and be forced to stand on the spot London claimed she was raped. Instead, Kenya kicked off her shoes and went up the stairs.

Barely finding the strength to pee, she let her track pants fall to the floor as she sat on the toilet. After unzipping her jacket Kenya practically threw herself in bed burying her body underneath the sheets. Since it was Monday and the club didn't reopen until Tuesday night, she settled in for some much-needed rest and an escape from reality.

Chapter 5

Da Mornin' After

London

The cloudy skies brought about more tears and frustration. It was mid-evening and London still hadn't heard from her sister. Not that she really expected her to call after the crucial bombshell she dropped the night before but she still held out hope. O.T. had stumbled in just a few hours earlier giving her an update on the Chocolate Bunny saga as well as informing her on the details of Paris. London, even though she hated his woman, was still shocked. When he said that he was gonna be staying in the adjoining room she wanted to tell him, hell naw! But since he paid for the suite, she really didn't have a choice. Plus at this point, she truly had no overwhelming desire to be alone.

In between the nasty, obnoxious sounds of him grunting and passing gas in his sleep and his loud vibrating cell phone, which was constantly going off, London couldn't think nor go back to sleep. Unpacking her suitcase, she made herself temporarily at home. Following a long, hot soul-pleasing shower, she wrapped up in the thick hotel robe and ordered room service for the second time that day. Staring at the phone that sat on the nightstand, she picked up the receiver and got an outside line. Slowly dialing the number, London rubbed her stomach waiting three long rings before the only friend she seemed to have left in the world answered.

"Hello."

"Hey! I need to come home," London cried.

Royce

"I wish that stupid idiot we running around here calling boss would just wise the fuck up." As the clouds darkened and the rain showers poured, Marco drove his green low-key van through a huge puddle of water that was starting to form. "That ho of his probably in Vegas soaking up the sunshine."

"Yeah, you right." His boy smoked a blunt and reclined his seat even farther as the long hours dwindled. "And he got us out here in a damn thunderstorm pounding the pavement. Twenty minutes more of this dumb shit and you can drop me by the crib!"

It was six forty-five in the evening and Royce had still yet to hear from Chocolate Bunny. He had every one of his crew on the hunt, checking afterhours spots, riding through the parks and staking out the mall and hair salons. Royce knew his woman was no angel, but she had a good heart with every intention of changing for the better. This baby Nicole was carrying was gonna be a fresh start for her and him. She'd finally have someone in her life who loved her unconditionally, never mind the kid was a forever meal ticket; and Royce, who was pushing into his late sixties, could prove to the younger cats who surrounded him that he was still very much vital and true to the game.

Having a young girl swinging from his arm, even if she was a slut, and possessing a direct line to Javier, one helluva of a strong drug connect, made him feel strong and infallible. Yet and still, not knowing anyone in Chocolate Bunny's immediate or distant family to contact he'd no choice but to sit idle and wait for her to call him. With the clock ticking and still no word, he called O.T. giving him the third degree for the fifth time.

"Yeah! Speak on it!" O.T. moaned.

"Hey, man, it's me."

"And?"

"Have you heard anything yet?"

"Damn, I done told ya the last time ya called and the time before that I ain't talk to her! I don't patrol the next nigga's pussy! Ya feel me!"

"This don't make no kind of sense." Royce waited for O.T. to feed off into his conversation. "Nicole wouldn't just not call. Not now anyway! It don't make sense!"

"I'm 'sleep," was all that O.T. muttered in response.

"Well have you at least talked to ya sister-in-law?"

"Naw, dogg! And I done told ya I'm 'sleep. Is you hard of hearing? Now if you wanna call Kenya then that's on you. But for now I'm out! Peace!"

Before Royce could even get a chance to say one more word, ask one more question, he heard the line go dead. Bad as he wanted to take O.T.'s advice and ask Kenya himself, he couldn't swallow his pride. She still despised him since their fight having him permanently blackballed from Alley Cats. Even though he made money and was a major player around those parts, the club was still technically as well as legally her turf. And just as Royce's old luck would have it, ever since Storm's complicated return from the island, Royce had no direct number for him.

Storm

I can't believe I banged London. Storm laid on the couch wiping the sleep out his left eye. *That explains those flashes of that shit in the kitchen.* Moving to the right eye, then stretching out his arms, he strangely started reliving the incident London was now calling rape. As the reoccurring memory of her foreign body squirming around to meet his every full-force thrust and of course getting tangled up in the fact of realizing he'd gotten some new pussy, Storm's dick stood at full attention and hard as a rock. He was in deep shit with Kenya for having sex with London, even though it was unintentionally, but that didn't stop him from being a man. *Damn, not only did I fuck sisters, I fucked a set of twins!* He glanced over at the staircase momentarily before slipping his hand down in his waistband gripping his manhood. As his fingers tightened and his stroke speed increased, caught up with busting a nut, he shamelessly imagined both twins sucking his dick. *Damn, y'all. Damn. Don't stop. Don't stop. Make daddy cum.*

Yeah, yeah, yeah, he knew he was wrong as two left feet and being a dog, but shit, the fantasy he'd concocted was all in the pursuit of him getting that early morning hit. Bingo! It was done!

With no regrets heading upstairs, Storm stuck his head inside their room where he saw Kenya's silhouette sprawled out in the bed. While she was sleeping peacefully, bright glimpses of lightning blinked through the curtains and the heavy rain knocked against the sliding glass doors that led to the balcony. He knew she had a long night and was worn out so he tried to respect that. With no intentions to wake her, Storm quietly walked passed on his way to jump in the shower. *Damn, she looked good.*

Not being able to help himself, he paused once again getting another hard on. The thin beige silk sheet that was once on Kenya's entire body had fallen to one side of the mattress showing him a clear view of her perfect ass, which had his named tattooed in blood red ink on her left cheek. He knew once again he was wrong, but as much as he fought the feeling he couldn't help himself. Dropping his boxers to the carpet the shirtless Storm climbed in bed with his woman.

Wrapping his muscular arms around her, he slid his dick in between the crack of her ass. Kenya was still fast asleep, but out of habit subconsciously poked out her booty to meet his every movement. Storm took that as an open invitation, flipping her over, sticking just the head of his dick inside of her wetness. Caught in her dreams and still exhausted from the night before, Kenya unknowingly moaned slightly as her body relaxed excepting all of Storm, who pushed harder. Panting and grunting in her ear he started fucking like there was no tomorrow in sight.

Yeah, London, give it to me! Storm's mind freakishly focused on Kenya's twin sister. *I know you want this dick, so open up!* He couldn't understand why that shit was making his thang so hard, but at that point he didn't care. *I'm about to cum! I'm about to cum!*

"Storm!" Kenya woke up coming to her senses realizing that shit she was feeling was not a dream. "What in the hell do you think you doing?"

"Hold on, baby!" He tried to keep his pace up humping. "Don't move."

"Nigga, please!" Kenya in a rage pushed him off her covering herself with the sheet. "Are you crazy or what?"

"Damn, babe, I was almost there. Lie back down and stop tripping for one more minute."

"That's nice for you, motherfucker, but it ain't that damn easy. Did you forget you had sex, naw, I mean raped my sister?"

"Naw, I ain't forget about that shit." Storm still had a hard dick, secretly knowing that was all he could think about this morning.

"Well." Kenya pulled the sheet off the bed draping herself with it as she stood up going to the other side of the room. "Now what?"

"Babe, let me take a shower, then we can figure all this bullshit out. I promise."

"Okay," Kenya agreed ready to put stuff in its proper perspective.

Five long, difficult, grueling hours of back-and-forth discussions, arguments, and disagreements, breakups, makeups, and finally some sort of a solution, the couple was ready to face London to hear her take on what truly happened. Calling his brother's cell phone to get the room number he and London were staying at, Storm waited for an answer.

"What the fuck is it now?" O.T. bellowed believing Royce hadn't got the message.

"Slow ya roll, boy! What's that all about?"

"Oh dang, my mistake, bro." O.T. looked at his watch. "I thought you was that fool buster

Royce. He keep calling stressing me about that missing bitch of his."

"Well, he straight wasting his time worrying about her. She ghost now!"

"I feel ya, but that junk was foul." O.T. tugged on his morning heavy dick. "Chocolate Bunny had some good head on her!"

"Well, now she ain't got no head at all!" Storm being sarcastic looked over at Kenya and smiled. "Dig, dude, I know it was fucked up, but I ain't about to let my girl do no time. No matter what!"

"Ya right." O.T. got out the bed to take a piss. "And I know Paris's dumb-ass would've gone bonkers if she had to do one day behind bars. She already nutty as five fruitcakes!"

"Well, dawg, let me get to the point. Where's London?"

"I think ya baby momma is in the other room on the phone."

"Cut it out!" Storm fell back on the couch. "This mess is crazy."

"You telling me! She been around here throwing up all night and half the morning."

"Damn!" Storm hated the chaos he'd created.

"Damn is right. What you gonna do?"

"Well first off, me and Kenya is gonna come over there to chop it up. What room y'all in?"

"Man, I gotta make a few runs, but don't come up to my room with that loud arguing and bullshit you and ya girl is famous for." O.T. laughed. "Trying to perform illegal abortions and shit!"

"Fuck you, nigga!" Storm laughed back at his brother's twisted sense of humor. "You's a fool!"

After finding out the number, Storm and Kenya started getting dressed. An hour and a half later, they were out the door.

London

London ran her fingers through her damp hair as she lay back on the bed in distress. "I can't take it here any longer!" she whined. "I've made such a mess of things."

"What happened?" Fatima asked her best friend.

"First of all, I want you to swear that you won't judge me."

"Come on now, London. You know we're better than that."

"I know, but what I'm about to tell you is gonna sound crazy."

"Just tell me," Fatima insisted sounding concerned.

"Okay, here goes." London exhaled. "A few months back, Kenya's man was drunk and came down to the kitchen where I was at."

"Okay, then what?"

London, feeling humiliation, continued. "He must've thought I was Kenya, because he grabbed me and threw me down on the floor."

"Oh, hell naw!" Fatima yelled. "You lying!"

"Nope, it's true. Then he raped me."

"What! What! What! Oh, no!"

"Yeah, Fatima," London sadly confessed. "And that's not the worst part of the story."

"How can it get any worse?"

"I'm pregnant."

"By Kenya's fiancé?"

"Yes."

"Oh my God! What did she say?" Fatima quizzed not believing what she'd just heard. "Is he in jail?"

"No, he's not in jail. Matter of fact, he's denying the whole incident even took place."

"London, that is so messed up! I see why you want to come home."

"Yeah, I know it is."

"But wait, you still didn't tell me what your sister said. I know she pissed at his ass!"

"She's so busy being in love she can't see or think straight. She said I'm making the whole thing up because I'm jealous."

"Wow."

"Last night I told her the truth about what happened and she kicked me out her house."

"And where is he at?" Fatima was pissed.

"He's still there with her."

As London and Fatima talked, making arrangements for her to fly back to Detroit, O.T. came out the other bedroom fully dressed with a smirk on his face. He took his keys off the dresser then rudely interrupted, not even bothering to say excuse me.

"Hey, girl!" O.T. spoke in a hurry. "Your sister and your baby daddy about to come over later to talk or kick ya ass." He couldn't resist clowning her. "But any way it go, I gotta shoot a move but I should be back before they get here so I can referee or at least get Kenya off of you."

"Shut up and get out!" London tried covering the phone's receiver so Fatima wouldn't see how badly she was getting disrespected until he finally left.

Chapter 6

Oh, It's Like Dat

O.T.

The intense pouring rain didn't stop O.T. from driving into a carwash and using the sprayer to rinse the terrible stench from inside of his trunk. After putting the guns in a safe place and throwing all the stuff he'd pissed on out in a Dumpster, he didn't get time to at least squirt some disinfectant before Kenya had called him about Paris. By the time he'd left the hospital and dropped Kenya off at the condo, he was done, wanting to do nothing more than sleep.

Purchasing a good damn near twenty wild cherry tree air fresheners out the machine, O.T. tossed them all in his trunk then sped off toward Royce's main re-up house. After him bugging the shit out of him all day about the last time he actually saw or talked to Chocolate

Bunny, he knew it was about time he saw him face-to-face to play the shit off. It would look way beyond suspicious if he didn't at least say something to the worried man.

O.T. listened to the radio as he plotted what he'd say. He had to make it somewhat good, but by all means believable. And thanks to Chocolate Bunny and her jaded past, she made it easy and convenient. If all went as planned, he was gonna lead Royce to believe that all along his woman was cheating on him, seeing some rich white dude from Cali she'd met at Alley Cats. And since Royce and most of his crew were banned from there, he wouldn't be able to dispute whether it was true. Besides everyone knew Royce was so caught up, so blinded, and so far gone behind Chocolate Bunny's pussy even if the lie was a 100 percent authentic none of his fake loyal soldiers would risk their jobs or position to be the bearer of bad news.

As he slowly bent the corner and pulled up two houses down parking under a huge tree, he looked in his rearview mirror seeing Marco, Royce's right hand henchman, standing on the porch smoking a cigarette. The loud, cracking sounds of thunder filled the air as O.T. put his game face on. Yeah, this was it. Not giving a fuck about getting his wheat-colored Tims wet and stained in the heavy downpour he got out the car and sprinted, heading up the walkway. "Hey, guy." O.T. nodded his head. "The old man inside?"

"Naw, dude. You just missed him." Marco blew the smoke from his cigarette out. "He just bounced."

"Oh, yeah?"

"Yeah." Marco kept it short.

"Damn, as much as he was blowing up a nigga's phone I thought he would've been here posted." O.T. studied Marco's expression to see if he could peep out what Royce's mind set was.

"Please don't tell me dude was on you too about that slut."

O.T. now had the answer he was looking for. Royce was panicked and his team was loose lipped. He took that as his opportunity to plant the seed and lay the groundwork. "Yeah, the old man say he can't find her."

"Just between me and you, O.T., that tramp somewhere on the beach sipping on some big, fruity drink with a stupid umbrella in that motherfucker!"

"Yeah, man, I feel you." O.T.'s plan was working itself out. "We both know Chocolate Bunny be doing her thang!"

"Dude, I'm telling you, I don't know what's wrong with Royce's mind. Maybe he got Alzheimer's or something." Marco thumped his still lit Newport into the wet bushes as his dreads hung over his face. "One day he on top of his shit then that dirty ho come around and he jumps all off his square."

O.T. stared out into the rain as he let the young cat get all his frustrations and complaints about Royce out in the open. *Damn, he's bugging and straight dry snitchin' on Royce!*

"Yeah, man. That guy so gone over that female you ain't never gonna guess where he on his way to now as we speak!" Marco, who normally never liked O.T. and the power he possessed on a day-to-day basis, to be able to speak to Royce however he wanted to without consequences, now seemed to act as if they were best friends since kindergarten.

"Where is that?" O.T. stayed brief with his responses.

"That old bitch nigga done broke the number one rule to this here game we playing!" Marco pulled a blunt out his pocket and blazed it up. "He straight pussy whipped!"

"Naw? Are you sure?"

"Hell yeah! He went to the damn punk-ass police for help!" He deeply inhaled then choked as he chopped it up with O.T. "He down there right now probably crying like a baby making a missing persons report on a slut who don't even wanna be found!"

This shit is about to get real twisted now that fool done went to the cops, O.T. thought as he listened to Marco get angrier and more disloyal to Royce as the showers increased, the storm intensified, and the clouds darkened. "Where you get them trees from?" He prolonged the spontaneous little pow-wow to see what other information would slip out. "They smell righteous. I need to cop some of that."

"Well yo, gimme ya number and I'll hit ya the next time the Mexican dude falls through. His ounces be tight!"

"All right, that's a bet." O.T. gave Marco his cell phone digits to lock in then decided to leave before he seemed too nosey. "Well, dude, I gotta be out. Tell Royce I came through whenever he gets back from his little adventure."

"Bet, not a problem. And yeah, until Chocolate Bunny shows back up you can just holler at me for the package." Marco was really feeling himself. "I'll be holding for now on out!"

"I'm good on all that, li'l man, just tell your boss I fell through." O.T. cut their conversation in the bud.

A now furious Marco, with burning blood in his eyes, watched O.T. run off the porch in the heavy downpour, jump in his ride, and skirt off. *Who the fuck he think he is to be ordering me around like I work for him?* He let the purple fill his lungs as he got higher and more delusional. *Shit, if things go as planned, in a few weeks, I'm gonna be the damn boss! Shit, maybe his boss!*

Royce

Feeling lost with nowhere else to turn, Royce, this time of his own free will, walked through the doors of the police station. Wearing a green and yellow pants suit that was soaked from the rain and a pair of two-toned snakeskin shoes, he went up to the front desk.

"Yes, can I help you?" The female officer on duty looked over her glasses.

"Yeah, you can." Royce nervously out of habit combed through his beard. "I need to file a missing persons report."

"Okay. First of all, how long has the person been missing?"

"Ever since last night."

"What time last night?"

"The last time she called me was at two-thirty."

"Two-thirty in the morning?"

"Yeah, when she got off of work."

"Okay, sir." The officer became judgmental as she took notice of all the gold bracelets and huge gaudy diamond pinky ring that graced his hand. "It hasn't been a solid twenty-four hours yet, but I guess I can at least still write up an inquiry. What's the person's name?"

"Nicole Daniels."

"And her relationship to you?" She wrote in black ink on the report pad.

"She's my woman." Royce looked around hoping none of the dudes he conducted business with saw him come in.

"And her date of birth?"

"Sometime in March."

"You don't know the exact date?"

"Naw, I don't."

"Well, what's her approximate age?"

"She's twenty-two, naw, I mean twenty-three."

"And you said this missing person is your woman or your daughter?" the shocked officer antagonized glancing back up as she realized the despicable and appalling age difference.

"My woman I said!" Royce took immediate offense to her statement.

"Well, are you sure she just didn't run off somewhere with some of her friends?"

"Yeah, I'm sure."

"Okay then." She giggled under her breath as she continued to gather information. "And where was she the last time you spoke to her?"

"She was in the parking lot at Alley Cats."

"Alley Cats?" The officer's demeanor took a serious, unprofessional turn. "You mean the sleazy strip club Alley Cats?"

"Yeah, if you wanna call it that." Royce heard a lot of commotion going on outside of the front doorway and once again hoped it wasn't involving any street colleagues he was aquatinted with.

The female officer, whose husband had left her and their three small kids for a young stripper who worked at that very club, grew infuriated. She couldn't believe that this drugstore-dressed pimp had the nerve to be standing in front of her being so stupid as to believe that a common pole swinger could be loyal to anyone, let alone his old behind. She contemplated even taking the complaint wasting taxpayers' money on foolishness.

"What's a number you can be reached at if we hear anything?" she grunted.

Giving the officer all the contact numbers he had, Royce crept toward the exit praying to duck back out as quietly as he'd come in. When the glass door slid open, two burly officers struggled bringing in a girl in handcuffs who rammed Royce with her shoulder.

"Get the fuck out my way, old man!" she screamed out.

Royce didn't want any added attention so he left without saying a word.

Tangy/Vanessa

"Dang, how could you?" Tangy recklessly stormed through the tiny one-bedroom apartment. "I was locked up ninety damn days behind some dumb bullshit you got me caught up in and you fucked somebody else?"

"Would you just listen to me?" Vanessa begged.

"Listen for what? You's a tramp! Bottom line!"

"Tangy, please!"

"Get the fuck away from me before you piss me off again!" Tangy slammed the kitchen cabinet causing a chalk sketching of the once blissful lovebirds had taken at the park to fall off the wall and shatter.

"I said I'm sorry." Vanessa followed her angry girlfriend around trying to plead her case. "Let me explain."

"What is it to say?"

"The car note payment was twelve days past due, the lights were about to get cut off, and I had an eviction notice. What'd you want me to do, be put out on the streets?"

"Naw, I wanted you to do exactly what you did! Fuck my little cousin's man!"

"I said I'm sorry!"

"You could've grabbed your dance bag and hit a couple of clubs before you went out like that."

"Yeah, Tangy, you right, but I needed the money real quick and O.T. looked out."

"Ho, get off his nuts and out my face!"

Ever since returning home from the hospital, Tangy was busy packing all her belongings. Having had enough of Vanessa time and time again betray her, she opted to end their relationship once and for all. Vanessa, on the other hand, was trying everything in her power to keep her woman at home.

"Is this your CD or mine?" Tangy fumed going through their music collection.

"Why you being so petty?

"What?"

"You heard me!" Vanessa knocked the disc out her hands and stomped it. "What about us?"

"Us? Us? Bitch! Wasn't you just with O.T.? Didn't you just have his nasty-ass dick inside you?" Tangy yoked her up slapping her twice in her face. "So get the fuck on!"

Vanessa held her jaw in pain as the tears rolled down. "I already let you jump on me this morning and I ain't hit you back, but you ain't gonna keep dogging me!"

"Oh yeah?" Tangy let her jealous fury loose for the second time that day, back slapping Vanessa across the room. Then socking her into the brass and glass bookshelves she started kicking her.

Ring. Ring. Ring. Tangy's cell phone started to go off bringing an abrupt halt to her rage. Knowing that it could've been the hospital with information about Paris, she went to the other side of the small living room answering the call.

"Yeah, hello." She panted out of breath as Vanessa lay balled up crying.

"Hey, chick, it's me, Kenya."

"Oh hey, Kenya!" Tangy grinned knowing the mere mention of that name would make Vanessa infuriated and pissed. "How you feeling today, baby doll?"

"I'm good." Kenya thought nothing of Tangy being affectionate because she always was. "Me and Storm headed out in this rain to take care of some business, but I wanted to check in. How's Paris doing? What's the latest?"

"Well, sweetie, the doctor moved her to a semi-private room so they could observe her and run a few more tests, but if you want I can swing by and pick you tomorrow up so me and you can visit Paris together."

Out the corner of her eye, Tangy watched Vanessa crawl in to the other room. She quickly turned her back against the wall so she could be ready when Vanessa returned probably with knife in hand ready to slice some shit up. After five or six minutes more of talking to Kenya, strangely enough to Tangy, the usually overly aggressive Vanessa hadn't come back out in the living room or even made a sound. Making sure to promise to call Kenya back later, Tangy hung up. A few seconds later there were several loud knocks on the door.

"Who the hell is it?"

"Police! Open up!"

"What!"

"Police! Open this door!" They banged harder as the frame shook.

"No, this stankin' bitch didn't call these hoes!" Tangy sucked her teeth smashing a glass mirror with her fist.

"Police! Open the door!"

Before Tangy knew it Vanessa flew past her, flinging the front door wide open and she was face down on the carpet, a knee pressed in her spine, being handcuffed.

"Oh, it's like that? How you gonna play me? You know I'm still on paper!" Tangy wrestled as the officers hauled her down the stairs roughly dragging her body through the wet, uncut grass forcing her to lie by the squad car tires. "Now you can get back with O.T., you dirtball skank! Fuck you and him!" were her ultimate vindictive words before they tossed her inside slamming the rear door shut. "Y'all both got it coming when I get out!"

Vanessa, feeling like she'd gotten revenge for that ass kicking and Tangy out of Kenya's grip stood smugly in the picture window holding a wet washcloth to her face.

When the officers reached the precinct intake center, Tangy's tirade and attitude had gotten worse. As she was being marched inside, the wild, masculine female bumped, mean mugged, and vulgarly cursed everyone in her path, even an old pimp obviously in distress.

"Throw her in the back holding cell until she calms down!" the female desk sergeant demanded. "I'll let the detectives deal with her in the morning!"

Showdown . . .

O.T. drove up to the hotel's parking complex just as his brother was paying the valet.

"What up, dude?"

"Nothing. Just came from out Royce's way. That buster already done went to the cops."

"Oh no!" Kenya worried. "That's fucked up!"

"You gotta expect somebody to look for her." Storm hugged his girl as they all went inside the lobby. "But calm down and trust me. They ain't gonna find her!"

Approaching the room, Kenya started to shake. She knew that when it was all said and done, London was still her sister, but now she had her man's baby growing inside of her womb. With anticipation building from Storm also, O.T. tapped his fist on the room door, informing London it was him. Scared herself, she cracked it peeping out before stepping out the way so her visitors could come in.

"I see you dressed." O.T. was the first to speak.

"Yeah," London muttered barely looking up from the plush carpet as she plopped in the chair.

Storm and Kenya took seats on the couch, while O.T. went to the minibar fixing himself a drink. "Well, y'all. Let's get down to it." O.T. turned his glass up taking a quick swig then placed his hand on London's shoulder. "My homegirl here is knocked up and me being her unofficial self-appointed savior wants to know what in the hell you two plan on doing about it."

Kenya was livid by the lack of respect he was showing to her plight. This wasn't easy for her. Matter of fact it was the hardest pill she thought she ever had to swallow. "Why you playing so much? This is my life!"

"Yeah, mine too." London gathered the courage to speak.

"Then talk!" O.T. laughed guzzling the rest of his drink.

"Okay then," Kenya obliged. "London, what exactly happened that night?"

"I already told you."

"Then tell me again."

London, for the first time in months was completely honest about her feelings. She shyly confessed the truth concerning Storm's drunken condition and his delusional belief that she was Kenya that late night. Letting her twin know that Storm was calling her name repeatedly when they were having intercourse, then blacked out, reassured Kenya that her man was telling the truth and really didn't remember shit. Although London maintained the fact Storm had forced himself on her and he was too powerful for her to fight off, she still accepted full responsibility.

And lastly as for the reason she didn't say anything to anyone, she explained that she didn't want to hurt her sister's feelings. Besides, after that night, Storm went back to treating her the way he always did: rude and ill-mannered. London dropped her head in shame saying she felt abandoned and isolated as she revealed an ultrasound and prenatal vitamins in her purse.

"Well, now that everything is out in the open and the big cat it out the bag, who's hungry? I can order room service." O.T. acted as if he was the entertainment for the night, but no one found him funny.

"Shut up, O.T.!" Kenya felt somewhat relieved that Storm hadn't deliberately betrayed her and London wasn't guilty of going behind her back fucking her man out of spite. It still didn't make the present situation any better, but at least she felt slight closure to where the true loyalties of the people around her lay. "We gotta now just call the doctor in the morning to make arrangements."

"Make arrangements for what?" London wondered. "I already talked to Fatima and I'm flying back to Detroit in a few weeks to stay with her and Brother Rasul."

"Oh, so you're gonna get the abortion there?" Kenya perked up glad that her sister had started the ball rolling in ending the mishap. "That'll work!"

"What are you talking about, Kenya? I didn't say anything about getting an abortion!"

"What the fuck is you trying to say?" Kenya jumped to her feet. "I know you ain't seriously considering having my man's baby."

"No, I'm not considering it!" London was now up on her feet screaming back. "I am having this baby. No matter how my child was conceived, God blessed me with this miracle! And not you or Storm is going to convince me otherwise!"

"Is you crazy!" Kenya, fist clenched, ran toward London ready to fight. Storm, who up until this point hadn't said a word, came between the sisters physically holding Kenya back. "Get your hands off me!" she demanded trying to break free.

"Kenya slow down and calm down. She's pregnant!"

"So damn what!" Kenya ranted with malice in her voice. "Tell her you don't want no baby by her! Tell her to kill that motherfucking unwanted bastard! Tell her, Storm! Tell her!"

"Kenya, stop! That ain't right! She's pregnant!"

"And?"

"And nothing!" Storm reasoned not wanting to take sides.

"And he don't want you hurting my little niece or nephew!" O.T. kept playing the role as instigator.

"Shut the fuck up, nigga!" Kenya was in tears struggling to get loose. "And, Storm, you better let me go!"

When he finally let his woman out his grip, she ran out the room and down the stairs not even waiting for the elevator.

"Damn! She pissed!" O.T. ridiculed.

"Yeah, I know." Storm put both hands behind his head locking his fingers together as he slowly paced the room. "This shit is fucked up!"

"I'm sorry." London finally directed her words to her unborn child's father while rubbing her stomach. "I didn't mean—"

"Naw, it's not all your fault," he conceded cutting her off. "After all I was drunk that night."

"Aw it's so freaking nice to see Mommy and Daddy getting along!" O.T. was being a true comedian. "Y'all having a moment! Dang, Storm, is you gonna go find Sadie Lynn and tell her she gonna be a grandmother?"

"Come on, dude, kill all that noise!" Storm's voice took a harsh tone when his brother brought up their drug-addicted mother. He was fed up with his brother's antics and needed him to focus. "I want you to stay on top of that Royce nonsense. I'm serious!"

"All right then, big Bro. Don't worry. I'm on it." He heard the stern demeanor in Storm's voice and stopped joking, especially about Sadie Lynn.

"Okay cool. Now, I need to get down there to the valet before they let her set my damn car on fire." He headed to the door, which Kenya had left wide open, then stopped momentarily gazing back at London. "Do you need anything? Because if you do, don't worry. I got you. I ain't gonna leave you or your baby, I mean my baby, hanging."

"Go on and jet, dude." O.T. stepped up. "I'm here. I got her."

Storm waited patiently for the elevator instead of taking the stairs knowing it was gonna be another long night at his house. He needed time to come to terms with impending parenthood. If he was gonna be forced to be a father, Tony Christian aka Storm, like most men, secretly hoped his firstborn would be a boy. The only obstacle that was sure to get in his way of being the so-called perfect parent was the most precious gift God had blessed him with thus far: Kenya. There was no way in hell she was going to let her sister have his baby!

Chapter 7

One Plus One

Tangled Webs

It was seven o'clock in the morning and Detective Malloy and Sergeant Kendrick were just getting in for the start of their ten-hour shift. The short-staffed police department had the team pulling double duty most of the time. When Malloy noticed the pile of new cases in the intake box, he couldn't believe all the disturbances that had taken place in the city since they were last there. The water for their first of many cups of coffee was just starting to heat up when Kendrick brought in his first prisoner that was in lock up.

"Tangelina Marie Gibson."

"Yeah, that's me." Tangy leaned back in the chair as far as the shackles would allow her.

"I see here you're charged with assault of a one Vanessa Sunderland as well as resisting arrest. You know you're in a lot of trouble don't you?"

"Yeah, well it ain't nothing I can't handle."

"Well, tough girl. Your records show you just got released a short time ago and you're on parole."

"Tell me something I don't know." Tangy wasn't scared of jailing it again. She considered it her home away from home getting three free meals a day and all the pussy she could eat at night.

"Well if Ms. Sunderland decides to press charges that would violate your parole, which is a mandatory ninety days."

"Oh, well." As she watched the cop place the call to Vanessa, Tangy sat back mad as hell that O.T. was gonna be getting in her bitch's pussy once more while she was gone.

Meanwhile Detective Malloy carefully read over the paperwork on a missing persons report and felt like there was something bizarre going on. "Well, I'll be damned! That's strange."

"What is it?" Kendrick asked waiting to get an answer on the phone line.

"You know Alley Cats?"

"Who doesn't?"

"Well somebody came in here last night claiming his girlfriend is missing. And get this. She works at the bar!"

"Damn, that makes two people supposedly missing."

"What's going on at that club?"

Kendrick held up his hand when Vanessa picked up obviously saying she was definitely gonna sign the paperwork.

"Well?" Tangy was on the edge of her seat.

"Pack ya bags, honey! It's ninety days for you!"

"Whatever! Take me back to my cell! And if you and Columbo over there wanna find out some shady shit going on at Alley Cats get at the fool O.T., that's y'all's best bet. Nine outta ten he behind the bullshit!"

Having another officer escort Tangy back to her holding cell to await being bused out to county lockup, Malloy went to work pulling an old file out the cabinet. "Remember that old lady who came in here acting a fool?"

Kendrick poured his coffee in a bright yellow mug and set it on the desk. "How can I forget? She called both of us and the entire department incompetent because we didn't have any substantiating leads on her only grandson Deacon McKay's disappearance."

"Yeah, that's her." Malloy shuffled papers. "Well, with this Nicole Daniels being missing also, that might give us enough information to really go over there and put the heat on Tony Christian."

"You might just have something there," Kendrick eagerly agreed as he raised his mug. "Even though I haven't heard much about him personally in the past few months, it seems as if his little brother has taken over the reins and pissed somebody off." He laughed referring to Tangy's last minute outburst.

"Whoever it takes for me to lock up to close a few cases, I'm doing it!" Malloy found Royce's number at the bottom of the page and went on somewhat of a fishing expedition. "Yes, hello. This is Detective Malloy with the police department."

"Have you found her?" Royce perked up not having a minute's rest for hours.

"No, not yet, sir. I just got the case. I need to ask you some more questions for my notes."

Grilling Royce, discovering his criminal record was as long as his right arm, he strategically played the namedropping game to see what kind of response he'd get. When he mentioned O.T.'s name to Royce you could hear a pin drop as the line grew temporary silent, raising several red flags to the detective. "Well if I hear anything pertaining to Ms. Daniels, I'll be in touch."

"Yeah, all right."

As Detective Malloy ended the conversation, he had a huge smile on his face foreseeing something big coming out of this case was in the near horizon, maybe a possible promotion. The rest of the day he'd eagerly devote to contacting Deacon's grandmother for additional information concerning her grandson's disappearance, running Nicole Daniels's name through the system for a background check, and then he and his partner Kendrick would take a special trip down to Alley Cats.

But Royce was left not smiling. Hearing O.T.'s name mentioned in connection with Nicole's untimely vanishing had him heated. Easing back in his favorite La-Z-Boy recliner, he thought about the words Marco put in his ear when he got back from filing the report the night before. The long list of things Marco repeated that had come directly out of O.T.'s mouth made Royce's blood pressure rise. He cracked his old knuckles going over and over them in his mind: Royce's days of being a boss were numbered; going to the police was a ho-ass move; he always wanted Nicole for himself; and if Marco wanted to jump ship and work for him the door was always open; plus a few other things Marco fabricated and threw in to make the shit sound better.

Royce was glad and felt secure in his position knowing he had such trustworthy people on his team like Marco that would pull his coattail to disloyalty. Hell, to make his lies seem even more official Marco even showed Royce O.T.'s personal cell phone number locked in his phone that he claimed was given to him to use when he was ready to make that move against his boss. Royce didn't want to believe it at first, but O.T. had been acting strange. And add that with the police saying his name, it became crystal clear.

Business As Usual . . .

Tuesday evening came and it was back to business as usual. It was now two hours before Alley Cats was due to reopen and things were hectic, which was typical. Storm, who hadn't been actively showing interest in the club, made the wise decision to come back. After all, he was the owner. Needless to say, he had to keep an eye on Kenya who was acting irrational. Although he didn't blame her one bit. She did commit murder and now had to contend with London having his baby.

Kenya and Storm decided, by her hand, to come in separate cars. Avoiding the kitchen area Kenya stayed busy signing for liquor deliveries and checking the schedule to see what dancers would be coming in when Storm entered from the rear doorway.

"Hey."

"Whatever." Kenya brushed passed him not even looking up.

"It's gonna be a long night. Now regardless of our personal shit that can be dealt with, we need to show everybody here that ain't nothing strange going on."

"All right, Storm. I'll try." She fixed herself a strong drink then disappeared in the girls' dressing room glass in hand.

"Good, that's all I'm asking!" he yelled out to her.

Boz and the rest of the security crew made their way in and got their detail assignments for the night. It had been months since they'd last seen Storm and were all glad to see him back. Twisting the caps off a few beers, taking them to the head, Storm and Boz sat in the corner booth discussing certain changes that needed to take place. Knowing that Boz was the last one to leave the club before Kenya killed Chocolate Bunny, Storm had to cover his bases.

"Dig this." Storm rubbed his hands together. "Me and you go way back and you always held me down."

"No question, dude," Boz affirmed.

"Well, I need you to do me a solid."

"Name it."

"Well when you left Sunday night, who was here?"

"I think it was Kenya and Chocolate Bunny." Boz thought back to that night. "Yeah, it was. I think some of the girls fucked up her tires. Her crazy-ass was waiting for a tow truck."

"Well check it." Storm leaned in sliding Boz an envelope with close to $5,000 in it. "If anybody asks, you and Kenya locked up and left together."

"Not a problem." Boz, who had a wife, six kids, and a girlfriend on the side, could definitely use the hush money.

"So remember, the last time you seen ol' girl, she was sitting in her car. Okay?"

"All right, Storm, but what about the cameras in the lot?"

"Don't worry. I got the tapes."

They drank one more beer then opened the doors for that night to a small group of business-men who were waiting along with a handful of others. Within an hour, Alley Cats was packed. One by one the dancers took their turns center stage, swinging on the pole, standing on their head, opening their legs and just about anything else they could do to entertain the rowdy crowd and make tips.

As a nervous Kenya sat at her usual spot at the end of the bar sipping on her third glass of white wine, she kept remembering the haunting look on Chocolate Bunny's face when the first bullet struck her. No matter how loud the music was, Kenya heard echoes of London saying she was keeping Storm's baby. Tonight wasn't her night and to make matters worse, the girls started arguing in the dressing room about one of them stealing the others regular customer.

Tipsy as shit, Kenya burst through the door yelling at all of them to shut the hell up and lower their voices.

"This needs to stop now!"

"She started it!" Jordan pointed her finger. "This ugly ho don't know about me!"

"Get your hand out my face, bitch, before I bite that motherfucker off!" the new girl promised.

"Kenya, I think it's about time you better tell this whore the rules around here! She green to this game!"

"Excuse me! What did you say?" Kenya placed both hands on her hips. "Please don't tell me what the fuck I need to be doing in my own club!"

"What?" Jordan, who was used to doing as she pleased, was shocked. "You talking to me?"

"Yes, I am! You seem to be the only one who's forgetting who the boss is!"

"No, I haven't!" Jordan bucked. "It's the same Negro who owned this son of a bitch before you came to town from Detroit thinking you all that, Storm!"

Kenya had just about enough of Jordan's sassy-ass gold-filled mouth. If it wasn't for her calling Paris in the middle of the night telling her about Chocolate Bunny being pregnant, most of the bullshit she went through wouldn't even have gone down. Now she had the audacity to get fly with her. It was time Kenya showed Jordan and any other nonbelievers who was truly running thangs.

"Okay, Jordan. That's it! You're really feeling yourself tonight, so I'll tell you what! You got about five minutes in total to grab that dirty G-string out your cottage cheese ass, get dressed, and raise the fuck up out of here before I smash your head into one of these lockers! I put that on everything I love in this world!"

Watching Kenya remove her earrings, all the dancers backed up against the wall making room just in case any blows were passed. Not one of them was in the mood to catch a black eye or beat down on the humble. Most of the girls remembered the class-A ass kicking Kenya put on Royce a few months earlier and hated the thought of being in Jordan's present position. Standing with a small wad of cash in her hands and a stupid expression on her face, Jordan looked in Kenya's face and decided it was in her best interest not to try her.

Instead, the always gossiping dancer got dressed, snatching her makeup case and bag and marched out the back room and up front onto the main floor where Storm was posted, taking her complaint about being fired to him. Blah, blah, blah! Unfortunately for her, it wasn't her lucky day. There wasn't no way on God's green earth he'd go against any decision Kenya made tonight! Jordan would have to suck this one up!

About midnight, when the club was at its wildest, Storm got called to the front door by Boz. It seemed that a small entourage of familiar faces wanted to come inside, but were being denied entry. With full knowledge that they were all banned from the premises, Royce initially asked for O.T., but was informed that he wasn't there yet. By the time Storm arrived at the front, a brazen, cocky Marco was trying to flex on Boz.

"Don't let me grab them nasty dreads and take you to school, youngster!" Boz promised with certainty. "And give you a nice haircut!"

"Try it!" Marco reacted not backing down with his homeboy by his side. "You don't want none!"

"Hey now!" Storm intervened. "What it do, Royce?"

Royce was weak, having not eaten for days, but had to come to Alley Cats and see if his woman showed up to work. He hadn't shaved in two days and his suit coat was wrinkled. "How you doing, Storm?" He extended his hand. "Long time no see."

"I'm well." Storm wanted to punch him dead in the mouth for all the dumb shit he was talking on the island, but sympathetically gave him a pass, especially after getting a good, long look at the shape Royce was in. He knew what was happening now was bigger than that so he played off his furious grudge for Kenya's sake. "How's life been treating you?"

"Not so good," Royce confessed assuming O.T. had more than likely told his brother about Chocolate Bunny's sudden disappearance. "Have you seen or heard from Nicole?" he cut to the chase.

"Naw, this here my first night back at the club." Storm threw up his hands. "But my manz been here. Boz, when the last time she was at work?"

On cue, with his arms folded still wanting to battle with Marco, Boz answered earning his $5,000 payday. "She was here Sunday night waiting for a tow truck when we locked up."

"Oh." Royce was sad there was no other updated news.

"Yeah, I guess she got into it with some of the other girls and one of them sliced her tires." Boz shrugged his shoulders as he walked away to frisk two men dressed in dark blue suits and freshly polished shoes.

"Well, can we at least come in and see if she shows up tonight?"

"Come on, Royce. You know Kenya in there and she be tripping."

"I feel you, but I don't want no trouble." Royce pulled Storm to the side. "I don't know if you know, but Nicole is carrying my baby and I'm worried."

Storm instantly thought about London who was back at the hotel room pregnant with his child, and felt for Royce. "Let me go holler at Kenya and smooth things out and I'll be right back."

Finally convincing her that it would be better to monitor Royce's thought process letting him back inside Alley Cats and lifting the ban, Kenya agreed. As Royce, Marco, and their boy approached the bar to order a couple of bottles of Moët they stopped, strangely enough, standing on the very spot Chocolate Bunny took her last breath. Kenya needed another drink and quick!

Time ticked by and most of the crowd had trickled out when O.T. arrived. He was buzzed and feeling good bobbing his head to the music as he moved smoothly up behind one of the dancers whispering in her ear. Doing Kenya's regular job, Storm was going from table to table making sure that the remaining customers were enjoying themselves and getting all their needs catered to. As soon as he spotted O.T. practically dragging the young newly hired dancer up to his usual table he tried to run interference. Royce and his crew were already seated in VIP and Storm wanted to make sure his sometimes off-the-hook brother stuck to the planned script. But as fate would have it that night another fight broke out in the club distracting his attention.

"Well, I'll be damned! Look what the cat done dragged in this motherfucker!" O.T. yelled wrapping his arms around the girl.

"O.T.," Royce acknowledged him as a toothpick hung out the corner of his mouth. "Where you been?"

"What you mean where I been?" a drunken O.T. slurred. "I don't work for you!"

"Who said you did?" Royce questioned not trying to make a scene.

"Then what's with the third degree interrogation and shit?" O.T. let the female go back down the stairs as he leered at Royce and his boys. "A nigga just got in this bitch! Let a brother get a drink or something!"

"My mistake." Royce backed down much to an infuriated Marco's dislike who got up and went to the bathroom. "I was trying to get up with you all day yesterday."

"Yeah, I know." O.T. had the waitress bring him a shot of Remy off the tray she was carrying and downed it. "I slid through there, but you was out," he announced with a grin on his face.

"Yeah, I heard." Royce doubted O.T. knew his ambitious protégé, Marco, had repeated his insults so he waited to see how the rest of the night played out.

"Damn! I gotta take a leak." O.T. grabbed on his manhood. "When I get back we can kick it about a little bit of business."

Royce watched O.T. like a hawk across the club. Seeing him briefly talk to his brother then Marco who was just coming out the bathroom as he was going in, the old man felt deep down in his old bones a conspiracy was going on. As he finished off his last drink for the evening he anxiously waited for Marco's return to the table so he could grill him on what exactly he and O.T. had just spoken about. Arriving at the booth, Marco wasted no time filling his bosses head with another gang of lies.

"Yeah, boss, he asked me was I ready to get on his team yet."

Royce leaned back in the booth remaining calm, cool, and collected as he studied O.T. the rest of the night. Even though he said he was coming right back to holler at him about some business, O.T. spent the rest of the evening talking with his brother and Kenya, who hadn't moved off the barstool all evening. When it was thirty minutes before closing time, Royce sadly came to the conclusion Chocolate Bunny wasn't gonna show up and decided to leave. Marco led the way as Royce and their homeboy followed.

"Y'all gone?" Storm nodded. "How was everything?"

"The service was good all except for that rotten dead snake smell in here."

"What in the fuck you talking about, guy?" Storm was at the end of his rope being friendly.

"O.T.!" Royce threw the ball back in Storm's court. "I thought he was a man of honor, but I see he takes after his older brother!"

Catching a "no more Mr. Nice Guy" attitude, Storm took his game off safety letting loose on Royce so the entire club could hear. "Listen, motherfucker. I let you come up in my place of business because I felt sorry for you and you have the balls to insult me?"

"Well I—" Royce wanted to reconsider his statement but it was too late for all that.

"Nigga, here's five dollars so you can buy a clue! Better yet, take ten!" Storm reached in his pocket peeling the money off his knot throwing it in Royce's face. "Nicole's slut-ass ain't want you! She wanted what she always wanted some dick and some dough! Some nigga probably banging that now! And you running all behind her acting a straight bitch! Be a man!"

"She'll be back!" Royce proclaimed beating his fist on his frail chest. "That girl loves me!"

"Yeah, you right, after the other trick's cash flow runs low. But I feel you, old timer! Chocolate Bunny do got some good pussy don't she?" Storm yanked on his dick laughing as his brother and Boz shook their heads in agreement. "I wouldn't mind some more of that fat cat my damn self!"

"All that's over! She having my baby!"

"Yeah, I heard!" Storm was amused. "I just hope you get a blood test, but then again, you don't have to take me and my boy's advice about your whore's fuck game, you can ask ya crew standing over there." He motioned to the side. "They both done tapped that monkey too! Ain't that right, fellas?"

Marco and his boy chose to say nothing to deny Storm's words. How could they? Every guy in town who had a dick that got hard had banged that ho and neither of them were any different. Now worried about being out of a job they lowered their heads following a pathetic and embarrassed Royce who turned around quickly rushing out the club's door. Marco made up his mind that Royce wasn't fit to run their crew or even his damn mouth.

"Y'all come back now ya hear!" O.T. stepped in the parking lot further humiliating the trio.

"You and your brother can consider all our business dealings over!" Royce vowed shaking his old finger in the air. "This is war!"

"Nigga, please!" Storm laughed out loud as he joined his brother standing by his side. "You just figuring that bullshit out?" The battle lines were now definitely drawn and Storm and O.T. came back inside the front door. Before going to the bar to have a toast to the old man's soon-to-be retirement from the game they passed by the same two customers dressed in dark blue suits who had come in earlier right behind Royce and his people. "I hope you guys had a good time." Storm still was playing the part of host. "And sorry about all the wild commotion."

"Don't worry about it," one of the guys answered with a weird smirk. "Shit happens!"

"Well, fellas, I tell you what. The next time y'all fall through, the drinks are on me!" Storm placed his hand on their shoulders. "I'll make sure y'all both get the VIP treatment with some of our hottest dancers."

"Don't worry, we'll definitely be back." The other spoke heading out to the parking lot getting into their car. "You can count on it!"

After starting up the engine the two guys shook their heads. "Can you believe all that madness that just went down in there?" Malloy rubbed his hands together. "That joint ain't nothing but a crime scene waiting to happen. Hell, we could've made a few arrests for solicitation the first hour we were there!"

"You ain't never lied!" Kendrick smiled at his partner as they left the lot. "But from the looks of things, we got bigger fish to fry. It's about to be an all-out war!"

"Yeah, and when it's over and the dust settles, we'll be right there to lock the damn winners up for a very, very long time!"

Chapter 8

Only Da Strong

99 Problems

One and a half months past and the dreaded drug dispute war was in total full swing. Different crews who weren't necessarily in cahoots with Royce or Storm were now feeling the heat. A special tactics police unit was formed to deal with the drastic extreme spike in the homicide rate as well as home invasions, multiple car jackings, and any narcotic-related crimes. With added pressure of security checks at airports, bus terminals, and the train stations, transporting and smuggling narcotics was difficult if not impossible.

But where there's a will there's always a way. Shit, you can never hold the black man down! They always make do. It's in their nature to be warriors! Now when a small-time dealer was lucky enough to mess around and score himself a semi-strong package, he'd cut it with every chemical, poisonous or not, that he could scrape up. He'd stretch the package as far as he could and still make the sale to the street zombies who were beating down his door.

Unfortunately left and right, dopefiends searching for that ultimate high were getting more than they bargained for. As the throwaway population took what they could get for a small fee, they paid a bigger price in the long run. Some would wake up from the near fatal blast, but most didn't. The county morgue was being overrun daily with John Does. They were the first casualties of Royce and Storm's ongoing beef.

Javier, the connect, sent several stern messages that he was not at all pleased he could no longer count on the constant revenue that Royce was sending him monthly. Because of the persistent war, his overseas shipments had been cut in half. It had gotten far too risky and no one wanted to be financially responsible for the drugs being seized and confiscated. The last half of a bird Royce was holding on to in case of a drought, he broke all the way down and was rationing out.

Most of his once well-paid soldiers had given up starving to prove a point and were now flipping burgers at McDonald's to make ends meet.

Storm on the other hand was almost 100 percent out of product. Every heavy hitter source the brothers knew was either locked up or out the game all together. After scheming with O.T. for weeks trying to find another good, strong, constant, and reliable connect they came up with only one solution. Storm didn't want it to come to that, but it had reached the point that they were all living off the profits made from Alley Cats. When he finally swallowed his pride and went to a still furious Kenya with the idea she went bananas.

"Why should I help you?"

"Why wouldn't you?"

"Well shit! Let's keep it boogie!" Kenya looked up from the book she was reading. "I can think of about two good reasons why the hell not!"

"What you want me to do, Kenya? I done apologized a million damn times! I can't go back and undo the bullshit!" He finished buttoning up his shirt.

"Yeah, I know." She bent the book all the way open waving it in the air close to Storm's face so he could see the orange cover. "It's like the title of this book say, knowledge costs! And I guess a bitch like me done had to cash all the way out to learn that crap!"

Storm checked his pistol making sure it was on safety before he stuck it in his waistband. "Man, you need to stop reading all them fucking hood books you buy! They ain't doing shit but putting that troublemaking Oprah, Lifetime movie, 'fuck ya man' mentality in your brain!"

"Naw, you put them thoughts in my brain by getting my sister knocked up! Then you begged her to stay and have your stankin' illegitimate bastard, so do what you do!"

"First all, I don't beg nobody. I ask," Storm insisted.

"Same thing!" She rolled her eyes.

"Kenya, you and me both grew up without our fathers in our lives and I don't wish that on no child. Damn! Be reasonable!"

"You done made your decision, so leave me alone! Can't you see I'm busy?"

"Look, I'm going to meet up with O.T." Storm was tired of the arguing they went through daily. "Just think about making that call. It's the only thing we can do!"

"Maybe I will, maybe I won't! But don't hold your breath!"

Kenya then curled up in the corner of the couch engaging herself back in her book as

Storm left out the door. As she read page after page of the fast-paced hood book as Storm spitefully labeled it, she wished she had as much conniving hatred rooted in her sprit as the main character in the novel, Zaria, held. If Kenya did, Storm's days would've been numbered and London's too, sister or no sister, twin or not!

The next day when she went to visit Paris in the mental hospital they had placed her in, she would have to tell her the nerve that Storm had coming to her with his problems. The fact that he was paying all the bills and providing the food didn't matter. The fact that he covered up a murder for her didn't matter. And the fact that he tried everything in his power to make up for his mistake still didn't matter. Nothing did. Kenya was on the verge of giving up. At any given moment in time she could pick up, pack her shit, and get the fuck on. She ain't have shit else to lose.

Whether or not she really decided to make such a drastic move, she knew she'd have to make that decision ultimately on her own with no help from Paris, who was fully conscious, but hadn't muttered a word since the night she tried committing suicide. The one-sided visits would consist of Kenya telling Paris all her troubles and Paris never reacting. Night after night Kenya prayed that the next time Tangy called her collect from prison she would have some encouraging news about her little cousin's condition and mental state of mind.

Across town, O.T. was getting out the shower. Brushing his teeth and throwing on a pair of track pants, he went out into the living area of the hotel he and London were still sharing and lay back on the couch. "London!"

"Yeah, I'm ready. I was just ordering the pizza."

"All right bet. Did you get extra cheese?" O.T. grabbed the television remote switching it on to the Movie Channel.

"Yeah, how can I forget especially after the way you clowned last week?" Robe clad, she sat down in the chair putting her feet up on the stool for him to rub. "They said it'll be here in about twenty-five minutes."

"Okay cool." He massaged her right foot.

Since the night Royce and Storm threw down the gauntlet declaring war, O.T. had been sticking close to London making sure no harm came to her or the baby. His big brother had asked him to do him that huge favor and he finally after coaxing agreed. Now he and London were just about as thick as thieves realizing how much stuff they really had in common. From watching old black-and-white movies to playing chess all night, they slowly created a bond and a regular routine that made Storm jealous.

Late in the evening after one of Kenya and Storm's famous knock-down drag-out arguments, Storm showed up telling London he wanted her to stay in Dallas so he could be a permanent part of his child's life. When Kenya found out what he'd done she was livid and wanted blood. But London was overjoyed that her baby would have a father in his or her life, even if that father was her sister's man. Now whenever he'd drop by, which was mostly unannounced, he would find her and his now possessive brother behaving as if they were the ones having a child.

Knock, knock, knock.

"That must be the food."

"Yeah, London, you right so go get the door."

"Boy, you crazy!"

"All right." O.T. jokingly pushed her feet. "You need to get ya lazy-ass up and get some exercise."

Taking his gun out the drawer just in case, he peered through the hole in the door. "Damn, nigga!"

"Damn, nigga, what?" Storm gave his brother a stupid look as he brushed passed him no sooner than the door opened. "Did you forget we were supposed to make that run?"

"Awww shit." O.T. rubbed his empty stomach.

"What's wrong, O.T.? Did they forget the extra cheese?"

Storm heard London yell out to his brother and tried to play off his envious disposition. "Hey." Storm walked into the room where his soon-to-be baby momma was still sitting. "What's happening?"

"Oh hey, I thought you were the pizza delivery guy."

"Naw, sorry to disappoint both of y'all."

O.T. went in his bedroom and threw on some jeans, a hoodie, and his Tims. When he came back in he handed London some money and got her ice water out the minifridge, setting it by her leg. "Sorry, babe, we gotta go somewhere real quick, but I should be back as soon as possible." He was overly apologetic about having to leave so abruptly. "And make sure you ask who's at the door and peek out before you open it okay?"

"Yeah, I will. Just hurry up and go so you can get back!"

O.T. reached over rubbing London's stomach which was now poking out. "Be back, little baby." Storm went out into the hallway and pushed the elevator button like what just went down didn't bother him.

Detectives

"Things keep getting out of control." Malloy had just returned from a closed door meeting with the homicide unit. "We need to get some kind of a handle on all this gang banging nonsense."

"Yeah." Kendrick slowly went through a huge ever-growing stack of papers on his desk. "I ain't had no rest in my own house in days. Shit, my wife and kids starting to wonder if I even live there anymore."

"Well, with all this manpower on these cases something has to give."

Kendrick opened the confusingly thin folder labeled TONY CHRISTIAN for what seemed like the thousandth time studying it cover to cover. "I don't understand this. It shows he has less than an intensive record for minor narcotics violations and a juvenile record that's been sealed, but other than that he doesn't have a violent background or even a speeding ticket!"

"Don't be fooled by the good treatment we get when we're at his club," Malloy noted. "If he and that lunatic brother of his knew we were investigating them all that VIP treatment would be out the window."

"I know. I was just trying to find out what makes his mind tick."

"Come on, Kendrick. Leave all that for the head shrink in the prison we about to send him to."

Payback . . .

Storm and O.T. jumped into the car and sped off toward Boz's house on the far west side of town. As the radio bumped kicking out some old Tupac, a distracted Storm couldn't take it anymore. Reaching over turning the volume down, he cleared his throat.

"Listen, bro. I know I told you to look out for ol' girl, but it seem like y'all a couple and shit."

"Huh?" O.T. was thrown off by the statement. "What you mean a couple? We just be chillin', that's all."

"Nigga, I done seen you just chill with females and it ain't nothing like what I just walked in on."

"Damn!" O.T. pounded his fist inside his hand. "I don't know what in the fuck you think you walked in on, but it wasn't shit going on! A nigga can't win for losing with you. First you beg me to stay at the room with her, now you telling me to do what? Act like she ain't there?"

"Naw, dude, that ain't what I'm saying."

"Then what the fuck is you saying?" O.T. was confused as to what direction his older brother was really coming from. "'Cause you got me all twisted!"

Storm felt like a fool but he'd opened this can of worms and had to get the bullshit off his chest. "It's just y'all two looked a little bit too cozy that's all. Shit, I ain't ever seen you and Paris that damned in tuned with each other."

"Dang, guy, first of all, you wasn't never really around me and Paris like that. And second . . ." O.T. leaned back in the passenger seat. "You bugging all the way out acting like London's your woman. I know her and Kenya look the hell alike, but you do know the difference don't you? Or is you still on that 'you was too drunk to tell' line?"

"I know she ain't my woman, but that's still my seed she carrying." Storm protested as he bent the corner speeding down on the freeway entrance ramp. "And naw, I don't want no nigga, you included, running up in that until my baby is born."

"Come on, bro, you think I'd be that grimy with it? Me and her just be watching old flicks! Is it a law against that?"

Storm realized his brother was absolutely right. He was behaving like London was his girl. As he glanced up in the rearview mirror, taking a quick look at himself, he hoped Kenya hadn't noticed how he'd changed his behavior. *Damn, no wonder she's been heated with me.*

Putting their talk on hold as they pulled into Boz's driveway and saw him step out onto the front porch kissing his wife good-bye, Storm got serious.

"What up, fellas?"

"What up, Boz?" O.T. hung out the window before opening the door. "You dressed like you ready to roll."

"For sure." Boz, wearing triple black from head to toe, approached the car and jumped in the back seat. "Them faggots ain't gonna know what hit 'em."

Parking the car in a mall lot and switching to an old school Regal, the guys headed toward one of the hideout houses that a chick tipped off O.T. about. If all went as planned Royce and some of his crew would get ambushed and paid back for shooting a couple of Storm's employees as they were leaving Alley Cats. They were considered civilians and off-limits to the ongoing war. All they were trying to do was go to work, make a living, and go home to their families. Instead they got some hot lead in their body and a quick trip to emergency.

"There's the house." O.T. read the numbers on the raggedy mailbox as they passed. "8087."

"All the lights are off upstairs. Drive around the block so we can check out the back part of the crib." Boz slid two 9 mms out his vest gripping up on the handles.

"Yeah." O.T. was in agreement. "That's where my homegirl said they be coming in and out from."

"All right." Storm bent the corner of the first side street he got to and tried for them not to appear so conspicuous as they scoped out the area.

Scouting out what the trio needed to see in the rear, then counting the number of vehicles parked near the house that were linked to Royce, they decided it was time to make their move. Storm was covering the door off the alleyway ready to blast any motherfucker who crossed his path while O.T. stooped down in the thick bushes in the next house over, pistol also drawn. Boz, both nines in hand, cautiously crept around to the dining room window where they'd seen the most movement through the sheets that were nailed up serving as the poor man's curtains. Waiting for the perfect opportunity he listened to them talk.

"This bullshit is getting crazy." Marco tried convincing Royce to give up the senseless war he'd got them all involved in over Chocolate Bunny who was still missing. "We losing manpower every day."

"Well recruit some more soldiers!" Royce's beard had grown long as bin Laden's and was totally gray. "Even if you have to go to the schoolyard to do it!"

"How you gonna pay 'em? Not to mention everybody in town's momma and they momma's momma know this bullshit war is over a female." Marco took a cigarette out the open pack on the table and lit it. "Don't get me wrong. I hate them mark busters as much as you do but damn! I'm missing meals over that bitch!"

Boom, boom, boom, boom.

As Royce, his right hand Marco, and three other devoted young members of the crew sat around hoping for some paying work they were shocked and had no choice but to hit the floor scrambling for their burners as gunshots roared through the windows without notice. The hail of bullets seemed to be coming from everywhere.

"What the fuck!" Royce dived, belly down, near the hall closet and cracked it open, crawling inside to seek refuge. Even though he had his gun in his hand he cowardly chose not to fire back protecting himself or his crew.

Marco, knowing it was now every man for himself, crouched on his knees ducking behind the oak entertainment center that was completely full of holes. As he watched two of the guys run out the front door and heard an obviously separate gun battle ensue, he made his move strategically to the other side of the now disarrayed room. Callously using the third guy, who was dead sprawled out in a pool of blood, as a human shield Marco rose up returning fire in Boz's direction. Letting off the entire round, Marco tossed his dead comrade through the already broken windows and made his way out to the front porch.

Out of bullets, with his gun still in hand, he jumped over the steel railing. Quickly observing O.T. at the other end of the block in a foot chase, Marco sprinted into a neighboring back yard, hopped a few fences making dogs bark wildly, and escaped into the darkness of the night.

Chasing the other guy after fatally wounding the first one who exited through the door, O.T.'s adrenalin raced as he was close on his trail.

Seeing the scared, barely old enough to vote youngster try to hide behind an abandon car, O.T. cornered him up about to pull the trigger when he somehow grew a heart. Thinking about the boy's mother having to bury her son as the unarmed teenager begged for his life promising to get out the game indefinitely, he gave him a pass.

"Get the fuck on, little nigga!" O.T. motioned with his gun. "And remember the day a real OG let you live!"

Most if not all of the gunfire had ceased when Storm entered the rear door of his rival's hide-out. A fresh smell of gunpowder and dust filled the air and all was silent. With each step that he took the floorboards creaked. Easing his way out the kitchen, he looked over to the windows which were all shot out.

"Boz! Boz!" he tried whispering loudly. "Boz!"

Careful not to step in the trail of blood that was smeared across the warped planks, Storm heard some movement from the back hallway. Turning his gun to the side, ready to take a nigga's life, he froze listening for the direction it was coming from.

Sniff, sniff. He heard what sounded like a small child crying coming from the closet. As Storm twisted the knob he was ready to fire.

"Your ass better come out this motherfucker if you know what's good for you!" he yelled before flinging the thin door almost off the hinges.

"Please, Storm! Please don't shoot me!" Royce's hands were folded tightly as he pleaded for his life. The gun he had with him was on the floor on the other side of the closet as if it was poison and he didn't want to touch it. "Please! Please!" His tears were so intense they seemed to soak his beard.

Storm heard police sirens off into the distance and knew he, O.T., and Boz had to get out of dodge before they got caught up. "You and your crew done fucked up this time!"

"Please, Storm, let me live! I'll give you all the rest of the shit I got stashed! It's in the top cabinet over the kitchen sink."

"Come on, Royce." Storm had a flashback to the island where Royce was being a tough guy. "Dude, you once called me a rat and thanks to you and all your signifying my best friend Deacon loss his life."

"That wasn't my call." Royce continued to cry as he negotiated to see the light of morning. "Javier made that decision not me! I told him he could trust you, I swear!"

"Well whoever made it, you the one who's about to pay for that motherfucker!"

"I'm sorry! I'm sorry!"

"Naw, don't be sorry! Man up! It's what true gangsters do in the end!"

Storm fired one fatal shot in Royce's head who slumped over into a pile of old sheets. He then ran in the kitchen and snatched open the cabinet door grabbing whatever dope he saw. Throwing it all in a plastic bag that was on the counter he slipped out the door where he was met in the backyard by his brother.

"Where's Boz?" Storm heard the sirens get louder as he threw the bag to his brother. "We gotta dip."

O.T. caught the bag and nodded his head to the side walkway of the house. Looking over in the small patch of grass near a rusty chain-link fence, Storm saw one of Royce's soldiers face down in a pile of broken glass from the window above and he wasn't moving an inch. Less than a yard away, Storm focused in on Boz lying flat on his back, motionless.

"Awwwww shit! Naw!" He covered his sweaty face with his pistol still in his hands running over to Boz's body whose eyes were wide open. "Fuck!" He pounded the concrete wall.

"Come on, dude!" O.T. yanked his brother's arm dragging him away near the alley gate. "He gone, dude! He gone! I already checked! We can't do shit for him now!"

"But . . ." Storm briefly hesitated hating to leave Boz like that.

"But nothing!" O.T. took charge of the situation. "It ain't shit we can do for him by getting locked the hell up! Now come on! We gotta bounce before the bitch-ass police get here!"

Detectives

"There's another call for us!" Malloy grabbed his jacket off the hook. "The officers on duty said they have four fatalities."

"Another four?"

"Yeah, Kendrick. And they also said two of them would be of particular interest to our case."

"Good, maybe this is the break we need!"

When the detectives arrived at the crime scene, which was roped off with yellow tape, a small crowd of onlookers had gathered. The news cameras were rolling and investigators were conducting door-to-door questioning of all the neighbors.

"What you got?" Malloy put on rubber gloves and pulled back the sheet on one of the victims on the side of the house. "Any ID on this one?"

"No, but I'm quite sure his prints and the other victim on the grass are in our system," a homicide detective spoke up. "But the other two fatalities don't need identifying."

Leaning over pulling the sheet off the other body, Malloy was shocked. "Well, I'll be damned! It's Boz! One of Storm's men!"

"What did you say?" Kendrick got closer with his notepad in hand. "The bouncer from the club?"

"Yeah, one and the same." Malloy covered the corpse back up wondering what really went down earlier.

"And if you think that's something, I advise both you guys to go take a gander in the back hall closet." The homicide officer pointed to the house. "It's a real sight to see!"

Being vigilant so as not to disturb the integrity of the scene the detectives walked through the sea of forensic officers and were surprised to see Royce, who was still regarded by many law officials as a major player in the game, dead as a doorknob with one apparent gunshot wound straight through the head.

"Live by the gun. Die by the gun!" Malloy taunted as him as his partner headed back to the station to figure out their next move.

Lost Friends . . .

The ride back to pick up the car from the place they had left it was a somber one. Now one more man, a good friend no less, was lost to the senseless war Paris and Kenya had started. Not knowing what exactly to say or do next, the brothers made the switch and headed over to one of O.T.'s female friend's houses to shower and get changed into the extra clothes that were in the trunk. Just in case the police were at his condo, Storm didn't want or need to take any chances. He knew they had to lay low.

Realizing that it was going to be extra hot at Boz's house, Storm had the female drive over to there to explain to Boz's wife about the tragedy that happened before the cops got there to deliver the dreadful blow. He had the chick reassure his wife and kids that he'd handle everything and they'd never ever want for jack shit. Not that it would bring Boz's wife any comfort, but at that point, there was nothing else he could say or do. Even through all her grief, Storm and O.T. knew she was a true trooper and wouldn't say nothing to the cops about who her husband had left with.

"It was that little punk Marco." O.T. paced the floor wanting immediate retaliation.

"How you know for sure?" Storm's body trembled from anger as he drank straight from a pint of Wild Irish Rose, which was the only thing the project chick had in her small apartment.

"Man, I saw those yellow stank mc-nasty dreads swinging around when I looked back at the house." O.T. hated that he had left the front door to chase those other fools down the block. "I thought Boz had the nigga!"

"You know what?"

"Dawg, please." O.T. took the bottle from his brother killing the last little corner off. "I already know! Marco gotta die!"

"Fuck his daddy, his mother, his bitch, and his firstborn!" Storm ranted as he reminisced about all the times his boy Boz had his back and had held him down.

Even when O.T. was doing his own thang nuttin' up out in the streets, acting a straight idiot, Boz stood by his side. If nothing else before he went to his grave he promised himself he'd avenge Boz's death.

Chapter 9

Reality Check

Kenya

Making herself a tuna fish sandwich on wheat bread, Kenya settled back down and read three more chapters of her novel before putting it away for the night. As the hands of the clock slowly moved, she thought about what Storm wanted her to do. It wasn't that it was so difficult to carry out; it was she was still pissed at him for choosing that baby over her. And in her way of thinking, why should she help him put food in that kid's mouth, even if it was technically her niece or nephew?

As she schemed on how to get him back on her trail the telephone rang. "Hello."

"Hi, Kenya, can we talk?"

"About what, London?"

"Is this how it's going to be between me and you the rest of our lives?"

"Um, is you still having my man's baby?"

"Why are you doing this?"

"Well, answer the question." Kenya wasn't letting up. "Is you still having his baby?"

"Yes," London firmly replied.

"Then, yeah, I guess it is gonna be like that!" Kenya slammed the phone down on the coffee table and went back to devising a plan to get Storm back on her jock. Soon she was fast asleep on the couch.

Ring, ring, ring. Kenya was awakened the next morning by the annoying sound of the phone. "Yeah, hello."

Finding out it was Tangy calling collect, she accepted the charges. Filling her in pertaining to the last time she'd visited with Paris, Kenya headed upstairs to ask Storm why he hadn't woke her up when he came in the night before. By the time she got to the top and turned into their room seeing the bed hadn't been slept in, she hit the roof.

"What the hell! Who this nigga think I am!"

"What's wrong?" Tangy speculated like she could really help Kenya from behind bars. "What's going on? Is everything okay?"

"This motherfucker ain't even come home!" Kenya's heart pounded as she went to look out the front window to see if she saw Storm's car in the driveway. "I swear I'm done with his ass."

Tangy took that as her cue and cruelly added fuel to the fire. "Storm just like that grimy-ass no-good brother of his. They probably somewhere lying up with some hoes!"

"Bye, Tangy!" Kenya hung up on her not wanting to hear that dumb shit and dialed Storm's cell phone. On the first ring he answered.

"Hey, Kenya."

"Where the fuck are you?"

"I'm with my brother."

"Oh yeah?" she hissed. "And some bitches I assume?"

"What is you talking about now?" Storm barely mumbled.

"Why didn't you come home?"

"What?"

"You heard me! Why ain't you come home?"

"Haven't you watched the news?"

"No," Kenya conceded going to turn on the television to see what was happening. "Why?"

Storm sighed. "Boz was killed last night."

"What?"

"Yeah, and Royce and two other cats, but I'll tell you about it later. Me and O.T. out in the projects."

"Okay, I'll see you when you get here."

Kenya hung up the phone and was in shock as she sat on the edge of the bed waiting for the newscast to come on. Tears started to stream down her face as she thought about Boz being gone. When Storm was missing, he was the one who held the fort down. He was Alley Cats' backbone. Finally seeing the news updates breaking report on the quadruple homicide, it all hit home. Wiping her face with tissue Kenya sadly then started to wonder what in the hell Boz's wife was gonna do now with all those kids she'd have to raise on her own.

Damn life was much too short. She thought, as she made the decision to stop fighting Storm and try to help him, that could've been him lying dead on the side of that house.

Detectives

"Well it seems as if we've got a suspect for the four murders." Malloy smiled elated that a break in the case came so soon.

"What's the latest?" Kendrick poured his first cup of coffee.

Malloy then stood up heading over to do the same. "Some geezer said he looked out his window and saw a young guy with, get this, long yellow ropes in his head hop his fence. He's on his way down now."

"No, he didn't! Is he sure? It was dark."

"Yeah, I thought about that too. But the old man has bright motion lights that illuminates damn near the whole neighborhood whenever you step foot on his property." Malloy laughed. "Shit, matter of fact the city has ticketed him repeatedly ordering him to remove the high-voltage lighting. So if he said he saw a kid with yellow ropes in his head and is willing to take time out and look at mug shots, I'm going with it!"

"Well it seems like we might as well go ahead and alert the fugitive apprehension team." Kendrick started thinking ahead. "The only one with yellow ropes." He laughed, mocking the old man's description of dreadlocks.

"It's Royce's boy Marco Meriwether."

"Yeah, I know." Malloy waited for the suspect's photo to print out of their system. "And my guess is he ain't gonna give up without a fight. So as soon as we get a positive ID, let's plaster this picture all across the news and see how long he last in the streets!"

New Beginnings . . .

Weary and emotionally drained, Storm came dragging through the front door of the condo. Nursing a cheap liquor-inflicted hangover and a splitting headache, he was met with the smell of turkey bacon, eggs, and grits coming from the kitchen. Throwing his keys on the table he stood in the doorway ready to collapse. He had the weight of the world on his shoulders. Now not only was he responsible for Kenya, her sister London, their unborn baby, Alley Cats, the mortgage on the condo, three car notes, and he had to make sure all of Boz's family's needs were taken care of.

"Hey, sweetheart." Kenya, for the first time in over a month, ran up to him wrapping her arms around his neck. "Are you okay?"

"Yeah, I'm good." Storm was surprised at the greeting he got but went with the flow.

"What happened to Boz?"

"We went on a mission last night and shit got out of control, but Royce got his!"

"Damn!"

"Yeah, and now we gonna get Marco next!"

"I can't believe all this is happening so fast!"

"Yeah, Kenya, it's a long, crazy-ass story, but bottom line my manz is dead." Storm dropped his head on her shoulder.

"Don't worry, baby. It's gonna be okay," Kenya reassured him stroking his hair. As she was trying to be nice and comfort him she saw the scratch on his neck and had to almost bite her tongue off to not trip.

"I see you cooking." He rose up.

"Yeah, I thought you might be hungry. So sit down and I'll fix you a plate."

"That'll work." Storm's empty stomach started to growl. "Just let me jump in the shower and get some of this project dirt off me."

"Okay, babe." Kenya smiled putting part one of her plan in motion. "And while you're getting clean, I'm gonna make that call out east."

"Damn, Kenya! That's good looking!"

"Anything for you." Kenya winked her eye.

Storm went upstairs and turned the temperature dial on as hot as he could stand. Stepping out his clothes he looked at his muscular frame in the glass door. As the water rushed down on his body he had to wonder what happened to change Kenya's behavior so quickly. Now, maybe things could get back to normal. He prayed as the steam filled the bathroom.

Brother Rasul

"Hey, Fatima, how you doing?"

"I'm well, Kenya."

"That's good. Is Brother Rasul around?"

"He's out in the backyard." Fatima acted as if she had some sort of an attitude for Kenya calling.

"Well, are you going to get him or what?"

"Yeah, in a minute," Fatima huffed. "But first me and you need to talk."

"Oh yeah!" Kenya wasn't stupid and knew where this bullshit was heading. "About what?"

"Well, I talked to London."

"And?"

"And don't you think you're being just a little bit unfair?" Fatima asked expecting an honest answer. "That is your sister."

"Don't you think ya ass need to stay out my fucking business? You must have me all the way twisted! Just because you my sister's little friend and Brother Rasul running all up in that don't give you the right to jump off into mines! So back off!"

"Listen, London is my girl, so that makes it my business!"

"Bitch, please! Go on back to school!" Kenya dismissed her. "And put ya man on the line!"

"That's right, Kenya, you said it correct, my man!"

Fatima hung up in her ear and didn't answer the three more times that Kenya tried calling back. Needless to say, there's more than one way to skin a cat. Kenya dialed Brother Rasul's cell phone and he immediately picked up.

"As-Salaam Alaikum."

"Hey now, Brother Rasul."

"How's life in Dallas? I've been following the news and wondered when you'd call."

"You know me like the back of your hand don't you?"

"Yeah, I guess you can say that, huh?" Brother Rasul grinned. "Now what do you need, little sis?"

"Well, you know Storm?"

"Of course I do."

"Well, I know you don't really try to get off into the other side of the life he's living but we need your help once again or we might lose everything."

"You said we," he strangely questioned. "I got the impression from Fatima you two weren't doing so well."

Kenya turned her lip up at the thought of Fatima's big mouth running about her personal matters. "Are you talking about that mess with London?"

"Yes, Kenya, I am." He was truthful and didn't hold any punches when speaking.

"To keep it real. Naw, I'm not happy about it. Who would be? But that don't have nothing to do with me."

"Come on, sis, it has everything to do with you. Now if you can promise me you're gonna stay with that man and forgive him and maybe your sister's transgressions then I can help him. Other than that I wouldn't feel completely comfortable making the introductions."

"Me and him gonna stay together and get married really soon," Kenya honestly promised knowing she was about to try to get pregnant. "But as for London, I ain't gonna lie. Me and her ain't dealing."

"Well, I'll pray things one day change for you and your sister." Brother Rasul respected Kenya's word and gave her the go-ahead for her and Storm to fly out east to Detroit so they could all discuss business face-to-face.

When Storm came downstairs to eat an elated Kenya hit him with the good news. "Hey, babe. How was your shower?"

"I needed that." Storm reached for the plate she was handing him and sat at the table. "Just like I need this here food."

Kenya poured him a tall, ice-cold glass of freshly squeezed orange juice and took a seat across from him. "I've got good news and bad news."

"I can't take any more bad news." Storm held the fork in his hand as he waited for the shit to hit the fan.

"It ain't like that. It's just that Brother Rasul said he wants to meet with you in person."

"Oh yeah? Now that's what up!"

"But we probably can't get a reasonable flight out of here until late next week." Kenya stood up standing behind him and started massaging his shoulders. "Is that okay?"

"That'll work." Storm's face brightened up as his dick got hard as a rock. "That'll give us time to settle a few other thangs."

One thing led to the next, and before the estranged couple knew it they were buck-naked on the living room floor getting that shit in! Sucking! Fucking! Licking and sticking! It was nothing too nasty for Kenya in her sneaky plight to get knocked up. If Storm wanted a baby so bad, London wasn't gonna be the only bitch to give him one.

In the middle of their afternoon sexual exploits, the house phone and both of their cell phones went off simultaneously bringing a sudden screeching halt to their freakery. Pulling his still hard manhood out of Kenya, Storm reached up on the couch grabbing his phone.

"It's the alarm people. Yeah, hello."

"Yes, Mr. Christian."

"Yeah, this me."

"This is Westmore Security and we need you to get down to your property listed as Alley Cats."

"What seems to be the problem?" Storm got up off the floor as Kenya waited anxiously to find out what the dilemma was.

"There seems to have been a fire on the premises."

"All right, I'll get right down there."

Storm scrambled around looking for his pants and shoes, but Kenya beat him to the punch and was already dressed with her purse in hand. "Sweetie, you need to lay low for a few days. Let me go down to the club and handle it." She was firm not willing to take no for an answer. "And if I need your help I'll call."

Kenya did almost eighty miles per hour getting down to the club. When she pulled into the crowded parking lot Kenya swerved by several fire trucks and the arson investigator who'd already been called to the scene. Peering through her windshield caused her to want to cry. The perfect paint job they'd paid thousands for along with the neon light marquee were completely charred black. The huge double doors had been ripped out the frame so the firefighters could gain entry into the interior.

"What happened? How did it start?" Kenya tried breaking through the gawkers.

"Who are you, Miss?" the inspector inquired.

"My name is Kenya Roberts. I'm the manager and Westmore Security called."

"Well, Miss Roberts." He held his silver clipboard in his hands. "We'll have to wait until the hot spots are cool before we can really make an assessment of the cause, but I can tell you that our men found some suspicious canisters in the rear of the building."

"What! Y'all think it was deliberate?"

"Calm down and hold your horses. I'm not saying that just yet." The man walked with Kenya to the far side of the nosey crowd. "I'm just saying, off of the record, you and the owner might wanna start being prepared to answer a lot of questions."

Damn! Kenya bit her lower lip wondering who in the hell would do some old fucked-up bullshit like this.

"One good thing, Miss Roberts, is that most of the main destruction is on the exterior cosmetics of the dwelling, but the structure itself is fine. As for the inside you have extensive smoke and water damage."

"Thank you." Kenya took his card as she went back to sit in her car and placed a call to the insurance company as well as Storm.

Sadly watching the trucks pull off one by one, Kenya got a pain in the pit of her belly. Since she'd been in town Alley Cats and all the people who worked there had been her life. Now it would be closed and worst of all Boz was dead. As the twenty-four-hour emergency board up team arrived Kenya got out the car to make sure all of the building was being secured properly. In the middle of her giving them instructions she was abruptly interrupted by two men in suits.

"Hello, Miss Roberts. It's a shame what happened. I hope you are covered."

"Yes, can I help you?" Kenya stepped back, unsure who these men were who knew her name.

"Can we talk to you a minute?" Malloy politely asked.

"About what? Who are you?" She did a double take because they seemed somewhat familiar.

"About this unexpected fire and a few other things," Kendrick said.

"Do you know who could've started this fire? Does your boyfriend Tony Christian or his little brother have any enemies that you know of?" Malloy jumped back in.

"Who the fuck are you?" Kenya put her hands on her hip and got double ghetto on they asses. "You can't be no damn fire inspectors asking me no dumb shit like that!"

"Miss." Kendrick showed her his badge. "We're from the police department and—"

"And what? If you ain't arresting my black-ass, then y'all can both get the fuck on!"

"You act as if you've got something to hide. Did you know one of your employees got murdered last night?"

"I think you two better get off my property before I call my lawyer!"

"If you keep running around with the company you keep you're gonna really have to call a lawyer." Malloy returned the insult before heading back to the car with his partner.

When the police left, Kenya nervously called Storm back telling him what just had gone down. After Alley Cats was boarded up securely, Kenya posted a huge sign that read CLOSED FOR REMODELING, and skirted off back to the condo to order the plane tickets for Detroit. In the middle of all the chaos that was going on, she couldn't wait to get back to the town she called home.

O.T.

Instead of going back to the hotel where London was at, O.T. decided to crash at the apartment that he and Paris shared. He'd been back and forth there several times to pick up the mail and maybe get some more clothes but not to stay. As he shoved over a bunch of junk on the couch and sat down looking at the small amount of dope they took the night before, he felt almost sick to his core about Boz losing his life.

He knew if his woman Paris hadn't been on that insecure, jealous bullshit, Chocolate Bunny would be alive, Royce would not have been looking for her, there wouldn't have been a beef, Boz would be home with his wife and kids, the connect would have still been pumping, and everybody would still be making that bread. But the way it stood now, there was no turning back. He and his brother and sister-in-law were all murderers and Paris was chilling in the nut-house.

O.T. barely closed his eyes when his cell phone rang. It was London asking him if he was okay. She knew she didn't have the right to really question him where he slept or who he slept with; she was just concerned. After speaking to her briefly the phone rang once again.

"Yeah, speak on it!"

"What it do?"

"Who this?" O.T. yawned.

"Y'all motherfuckers tried to get down last night, huh? That ambush shit was real slick!"

"Nigga, what?"

"Yeah, but a pimp like me too slick for y'all!" It was obvious to O.T. that it was Marco on the line trying to go for bad. "But dig, I do wanna thank you for putting that old dog Royce out his misery. If I would've heard him whine about that dick sucker broad of his anymore I would've put one in his head my damn self! So straight-up good looking on that! I might let you and your brother live one more extra day for the favor!"

"You's a tough guy over the phone and shit, but you can trust when I run up on you, you's good as dead!"

"Oh you mean dead as that slow-moving, can't dodge a bullet goon, Boz?" Marco laughed showing no respect. "That fool hit the ground like an old sack of potatoes. Maybe I should go fuck his wife and play daddy to them kids of his!"

"You's a dead man!" O.T. vowed. "You betta watch over ya shoulder everywhere you go and hope the ho-ass cops catch up to you before I do!"

Marco confidently blazed up a blunt and sat back amused with O.T.'s threats. "I don't give a sweet fuck how many times they flash my picture on the news, them bitches ain't gonna get with me! Shit!" he choked. "Or you neither! And by the way, tell your brother's woman she looked fly as hell in the parking lot of Alley Cats."

"What?" O.T. furiously kicked the coffee table over in an insane rage. "What you say, nigga?"

"Next time I'm gonna burn that spot down to the ground!" Marco swore. "And p.s., you faggot! That package y'all took, hell ya might get a few stacks out of it but real talk it got so much cut on it y'all's dopefiend momma who I watched a dog fuck her in the ass this morning couldn't snort it! I had to give her old ass three whole extra dollars to suck my dick, too! Cash!"

"Bitch nigga, shut the fuck up!"

"Damn, O.T.! I told ya momma that same shit when she was on her knees choking on this big black monster!"

"Keep talking, but just know ya days are numbered!"

Since he'd called anonymous O.T. had no way to call him back when he hung up, but it didn't matter. Sooner or later the two would meet again.

Chapter 10

I Rep Detroit!

With two months past since the drought was in effect, things were still at a desperate stage for the brothers. The fact that Royce was now out of the picture and his team disbanded meant nothing to the amount of pressure by officials and lawmakers that was still on strong to stop any narcotics from entering their city and neighboring communities. Storm and O.T. alike had both been hauled off to the police station for questioning, but any small, minute evidence they had linking them to any crime was just speculation at best.

The only real other problem or inconvenience the brothers faced was Marco, who was still on the warpath trying to get some vigilante retaliation street justice for a drug battle that was buried with Royce. Although O.T. and Storm knew Marco was on the top of their list of fools that had to go to an early grave, negotiations still had to be made in Detroit so they could maintain the lifestyle that they wanted.

Landing safely at Detroit Metro Airport, Storm and Kenya claimed their luggage and headed to Hertz to rent a car for the short duration of their stay. Kenya had a lot of places she wanted to show Storm on his first visit to Motown and they needed their own transportation. With Kenya behind the wheel, the couple cruised down I-94 and were soon crossing into the city limits.

"Welcome to Detroit, huh?" Storm quickly read the green and white sign they passed. "As much killing that go on here, can't nobody feel welcome."

"All right, boy! Don't be talking about my city!"

"I mean goddamn, Kenya, I ain't mad at you!" Storm laughed as he sat back observing all the blight that surrounded them every block they drove. "If I grew up in a city with all these casinos, a police department that ain't trying to catch a cold, let alone a criminal, crackheads stealing copper pipes in broad daylight pushing them in shopping carts and of course, a hip hop mayor who just got arrested and convicted, I'd be sticking up for my town too!"

"Forget you!" Kenya rolled her eyes amused at Storm's sarcastic remarks. "Dallas ain't much better!"

"I hear ya talking!" Storm laughed at the raggedy roads.

Checking into the hotel inside of the Motor City Casino, Kenya and Storm made love on top of the bed, not bothering to even pull back the covers. Hadn't shit changed for Kenya whose main agenda was to still trying to get pregnant. Time after time, nut after nut, she prayed Storm's seed was in her.

Taking a quick shower then getting dressed Kenya stood looking out the huge window toward downtown. Gazing at the cars flying past on the freeway she couldn't help but wonder how a chick from "the D" got caught up in the middle of so much foolishness. Nevertheless here she was, back in the town she happily left, trying to help her man survive in the game.

"You ready, babe, or what?"

"Yeah, let's roll." Storm was anxious to see more of the city and of course meet Brother Rasul, who was preoccupied at the mosque. "I'm starving. Let's hit that all-ya-can-eat spot you been bragging about in this joint."

Eating until they thought they'd both burst at the buffet, Kenya and Storm jumped in their rental and headed to the northwest side of town. Exiting onto Seven Mile from the Lodge Freeway they made a quick left, then another left onto Sussex Street, turning into Brother Rasul's modest bungalow-style home. Storm looked back in the driveway seeing a brand new car and a Ninja-style motorcycle parked near the deck. Making sure he was completely aware of his surroundings he low key glanced up noticing the security cameras inconspicuously placed at every point of entry.

This black man ain't messing around, Storm thought as he and Kenya waited patiently on the front porch for the famous Brother Rasul who his girl idolized. Hearing all the deadbolt locks turn they were finally face to face.

"As-Salaam Alaikum."

"Brother Rasul!" Kenya jumped up hugging her constant savior. "I missed you! I missed you!"

"How you doing, Brother?" Storm cordially greeted him as Kenya smiled from cheek to cheek.

"I'm good. How about yourself?"

Storm firmly shook his huge hand as he sized him up. *Damn, this nigga bigger than Boz!* "I'm well."

"Come on in and have a seat." Brother Rasul was cordial as he made sure they were comfortable. "How was your flight?" He directed his attention to Storm. "I hope it was not too much inconvenience on the trip."

"It was good. I'm just glad to be here and finally meet you. Before we go any further, I want to thank you personally for your assistance concerning Javier."

"Not a problem." Brother Rasul was gracious. "As you can see considering the reason for your visit, I'd do anything for Kenya. Matter of fact, I know you two just got here, but I bet you're anxious to get down to business."

Kenya excused herself going to pick up a carryout order from a Jamaican restaurant nearby giving the men a chance to talk. By the time she returned with Brother Rasul's lunch, which consisted of goat and stewed vegetables, the deal had been struck and all was well. Spending a few more hours reminiscing about their past and who was doing what, Kenya and Storm said their good-byes and left for the evening.

Brother Rasul had carefully grilled Storm about his business dealings as well as his personal life. He always felt that if a man couldn't take care of his household, he certainly couldn't maintain any other business outside of that. But finding out Storm was willing to step up and take care of his responsibilities as far as with his and London's child and still seemed to love and care for Kenya made all the difference. Despite opposition from Fatima for helping Kenya, he was confident he was making the right decision. So while eating his food that had to be warmed up, Brother Rasul sat at his table figuring out which one of his immediate trusted associates would be the direct pipeline for Kenya's man.

London

Growing closer as the days past, O.T. and London slowly started to develop feelings for one another that could be only considered borderline love. Even though the two tried to fight it, night after night it grew stronger. As London's stomach got bigger indicating the baby's arrival date was narrowing down, she didn't have any maternity clothes that would fit her. Instead of turning to Storm, she turned to O.T. who couldn't wait for the baby to be born. With his brother and Kenya, who had still been alienating London, out of town in Detroit, O.T. rushed back to the hotel suite they were still calling home to take London to the mall.

"Hey, girl!" O.T. yelled out. "You about ready?"

"Yes, here I come." London was excited to get out and get some fresh air. Other than the trips she made to the doctor, the single expectant mother rarely stepped foot outside of the room.

As she slightly wobbled to the elevator and out to the car, O.T. proudly held her arm like they were husband and wife. Arriving at the mall, he pulled up in valet paying the attendant to park his whip up front.

"How you doing, Miss Kenya?" the man mistook London for her sister who was a frequent visitor to the mall.

Neither she nor O.T. spoke up to correct the attendant as they breezed inside the doors and strolled hand in hand through the air conditioned mall. Most of the salespeople repeated the same mistake as London felt what it was like to be Kenya. Bogged down with several huge bags at her side, London sat in the food court sipping on a fruit smoothie as O.T. went to the bathroom.

"Wow, Kenya! Congratulations on the baby!" The lady from the cosmetics store smiled. "We're having a sale this weekend for our VIP customers! Hope to see ya there!"

"Hey, Kenya! Damn!" one of the dancers from the club spoke as she walked by with some nerdy old trick who was obviously sponsoring her shopping spree. "You and Storm been busy I see making that baby. Don't forget to call me as soon as y'all finish remodeling! I'm ready to get back to work! Ain't no club like Alley Cats!"

London didn't say a word because the sleazy-dressed female was half correct: she and Storm were having a child. She just sat back and nodded, amused that not one of the people who seemed to worship her twin could tell them apart. It was just like being back in grade school deceiving the teachers.

"Oh I see you and that ho-ass motherfucker Storm having a kid huh?" a young guy with a tight-fitting baseball cap, a ponytail, and wire-rimmed glasses spewed quickly walking by dropping a business card from the hotel she and O.T. were staying at in her lap. "Tell him ain't shit changed. I'm still on that ass!"

O.T. had just zipped his pants up as his cell phone rang. "Yeah, speak on it!"

"What's up, bitch?"

"Nigga, stop calling my phone! Before I—"

"Before you do what?" Marco gloated. "Ain't shit changed between me and you and that pretty boy brother of yours!"

"Then stop hiding like a punk and come the fuck out and play with the big dogs!"

"Oh you mean like you been playing house and acting all the fuck in?" Marco grinned. "Tell me one thang. Do your big brother know how touchy feely you and his pregnant ho been acting all day in the mall, holding hands and shit?"

"Nigga, what?" O.T. ran out the bathroom realizing that Marco couldn't be that far to know what moves he and London had made.

"Oh I see you done taking a leak huh?" Marco hung the payphone up he'd called from and exited out a side door driving away in a broken-down low-key car.

"Hey, babe! You okay?" O.T. ran to London touching her face.

"Yeah, I'm good, but some idiot came by threatening Storm and gave me this card from the hotel."

When O.T. saw that the card he immediately realized his number one enemy had been trailing him, not only today but for some time now. While he was busy secretly falling in love with his brother's baby momma, Marco was doing his homework like a true gully solider at war. It was now getting beyond crucial and time he got back in the streets and handled ol' boy once and for all. At that point he called Storm who was still out of town informing him that for safety precautions he and London would be relocating ASAP.

Storm

Taking in all the late-night wild-out sights Detroit had to offer filled with Negroes rocking big block gators and bitches with three packs of weave, Storm had a ball. Before he and Kenya finally got ready to leave the Motor City they visited a few of Kenya's old friends, including Young Foy who was raising her friend Raven's son. Lastly and most importantly the pair went to pay their respects at her uncle's and grandmother's gravesites.

Sitting in the terminal waiting for their delayed flight to board, Storm's cell phone rang. Glancing at the caller ID he was glad that it was O.T. checking in.

"What up, doe?" Storm laughed nudging Kenya as he mocked the way Detroiters greeted each other.

"Damn, where you pick that ol' country-sounding bullshit up at?"

"Yeah, bro." Storm checked his watch. "These niggas in the D is off the fucking chain! I'll give 'em they props, they is some straight-up killers! Shit, a couple of young'uns I seen last night at this spot here called Chandler Park need to fly out to Dallas and get on our team!"

"Not to cut you off but . . ." O.T.'s voice was solemn.

"But what? Is everything okay with baby?"

When Kenya heard him say the word "baby" her ears perked up shamefully hoping that her sister had suffered a miscarriage. As soon as Storm got off the phone, the loudspeaker announced that they were finally boarding stopping Kenya from being nosey. Within five minutes of the plane taking off, Storm reached over holding her hand looking serious as a motherfucker.

This is it! This nigga about to say that baby dead! Kenya's mind was working overtime. *Say it! Say it!*

"Listen, sweetie." Storm rubbed her hand. "I need to say something to you."

Here it comes! Say it! Say it so this nightmare can be over!

"Before we took off O.T. called and said that there was a problem at home."

Kenya nodded her head as she frowned. "Oh yeah?"

Storm knew that she was gonna go bananas when he told her what he and O.T. decided but there was no other solution. "Yeah, well, you know we got people out pounding the pavement looking for that ho-ass buster Marco who killed Boz and set the fire."

"I know." Kenya sat back in her seat wondering where all this shit was going. "And?"

"Well, your sister and O.T. were out at the mall and it seems like Marco was following them." Storm wrung his hands together as he tried whispering. Things had been going so good between them the last week or so he hated to ruin it with what he was about to say. "So me and O.T. thought it would be better if he and London moved from the hotel."

"So? I don't understand." Kenya gritted her teeth as she talked under her breath and held onto her purse tightly pressing it close to her breast. "What that shit got to do with me?"

"Calm down." Storm placed his hand on her knee in hopes of her being quiet. "Just wait a minute."

"Okay, I'm calm, so speak."

"Bottom line is, they both gonna stay with us at the condo!"

"Oh hell naw!" Kenya unfastened her seat belt, leaped to her feet, and screamed, causing other passengers to get scared.

"Sit down and shut the fuck up before you get me and you arrested by the damn FBI or something!" He snatched her back in her seat.

After that outburst the stewardess came to check that everything was okay with the couple. Kenya silently pouted waiting until they landed to get back off into Storm's black ass.

I don't know who this nickel slick nigga think he playing with! After I hooked him up with my people he think he just gonna dog me like that! Humph, we'll see who gonna get the last laugh when I get that connect cancelled! She continued to squirm as she vindictively rolled her eyes calculating her next move. *Watch! As soon as we touch down I'm packing all my stuff and moving the fuck out! He can have that backstabbing tramp! I should have just left that no-good motherfucker on that island instead of jacking off my retirement stash! I look too good for all this foul-ass bullshit to be happening to me! Ain't shit changed! I can still get any nigga I want! Storm gonna regret fucking me over!*

Chapter 11

Home Sweet Home

Old Ghost

"You just about packed?"

"Yeah, O.T., but do you think this is a good idea?"

"Don't worry about it." He gathered all their belongings stacking them up by the door. "Storm is taking care of all that madness and Kenya is gonna go for it."

"Yeah, but I can't believe my sister is gonna let me and my baby back in her house." London protectively stared downward rubbing her belly. "She's still mad at me."

"It's all good. Her and Storm is still in Detroit handling some business," O.T. confirmed. "By the time they get back later tonight we'll be already settled in."

"Still, I don't know."

When the bellman came with the handcart to take their entire luggage down to the car O.T. did one more quick sweep of the room to ensure they hadn't left anything. Standing on the elevator London worried if she was doing the right thing moving back under the same roof as her sister's fiancé. Even though she had developed strong undeniable feelings for O.T., the fact that Storm's baby was now moving and kicking drew her emotionally toward him.

"Listen up, girl, that's the best place for us all to be chillin' at right now," O.T. lectured. "If that asshole Marco shows up anywhere near the condo, he'll stick out like Uncle Luke in a camp filled with sissies! Plus, I know for a fact he knows where my and Paris's apartment is so that's definitely out of the question!"

"All right then," London finally conceded.

Homecomings . . .

"Now are we clear about why they're staying at the condo with us?"

"Storm." Kenya smirked. "They staying with you! I already done told you I'm out!"

"Why it gotta be like that?"

"Whatever! All three of y'all can starve together!"

"What you trying to say?"

"Trying? I done said it!" Kenya looked at the Dallas skyline as they drove. "I'ma do me!"

It didn't take being a rocket scientist for Storm to figure out his deal with Brother Rasul was about to be axed. He knew he needed that connect so he tried to do damage control. What he was about to say was the honest truth.

"Baby, I love you and always will. When I gave you that ring, I meant it. You're the one I want. Nobody can take your place."

"Oh yeah?" Kenya was starting to soften up as Storm caressed her hand. "Are you sure?"

"Yes, Kenya, I'm positive. The only reason I wanted London to move back in with us is to make sure nothing happens to my son."

"Your what!" Kenya screamed snatching her hand away from his. "What you mean son? How in the fuck you know what the bastard is?"

Storm had dropped the ball and had to fess up. "First of all stop calling the baby a bastard. And secondly, I know it's gonna be a boy because I saw the ultrasound pictures."

"And how in the fuck did you see that?" Kenya got to going on him.

"All right, Kenya, I ain't gonna lie!" Storm rubbed his chin as he turned the corner less than a mile from the condo. "I went to the doctor with her a couple of times and that's when I saw it."

"You son of a bitch!" Kenya reached over slapping his face. "You ain't shit!"

Storm touched his cheek and smiled. "I'll tell you what. I probably had that coming so fuck it. But it still don't change the fact that you need to grow the hell up, face the reality of the situation, and get yourself in check!" he advised. "Because London and O.T. already moved in. They're probably at the house now."

Ten minutes later Storm turned into the driveway. As Kenya looked over at the condo seeing lights illuminating in the house that she hadn't left on, she remembered the night she and London returned from Detroit to find her home destroyed, Storm missing, and Deacon's headless torso floating in the tub.

Chapter 12

Cloak and Dagger

Marco

"You should've seen that bitch-ass nigga run up out the bathroom when he thought his brother's woman was in danger." Marco lay back talking smack on the couch of his boy's apartment. "But keeping it boogie, I could've stomped a patch of meat out that female's scalp just like I did that project slut who snitched me out to O.T."

"Then why didn't you?" Coonee coughed passing the blunt back to his manz. "That bitch had it coming, just like her people. Shit, on the for real, my nigga, that's why we sitting in this motherfucker now on craps eating bologna and cheese sandwiches!"

Marco inhaled deeply. "You know that wannabe bossy chick is pregnant."

"So what! Is it your kid?"

"Hell naw!"

"Then fuck that bitch, right!"

"Yeah, you right, Coonee, but if you could've seen her face when I ran up on her," Marco joked passing the blunt back. "I damn near scared the ho into labor! Kenya was shook and acted like she didn't know who in the hell I even was!"

"Yeah, well, Marco, as hot as the police is on ya trail, that might've been ya last chance to get at her."

"Naw, dude, believe me when I tell you. It ain't never too late. I'm on top of they every move!"

Police

Malloy and Kendrick had been conducting several investigations that were all somehow or other linked into Deacon McKay's and Nicole Daniels's disappearances. Sitting behind their desks the officers sighed annoyed that they were now getting chewed out by an old lady for not doing their jobs properly.

"I've been coming down here to this police station month after month and you two young men haven't told me not one single thing about my missing grandson." Mrs. McKay's wrinkled fingers clutched her Bible. "I don't understand what this world is coming to. Nobody knows anything! That club he used to be at is burned up and now I can't even find that no-good supposed to be best friend of his Tony or that crazy-talking brother E.T., Q.T., O.T., ABC, or whatever his name is."

"Well, Mrs. McKay, we've been doing our best to follow any leads that come in." Kendrick tried comforting the older woman. "But it seems none of them pan out to be creditable."

Once again Mrs. McKay left the station with no answers to her agonizing plight for closure.

"We've gotta put an end to all this madness in this town once and for all," Malloy interjected picking up the phone. "I'm gonna put a tail on Tony Christian and his little brother and see where that takes us."

"Yeah." Kendrick was in agreement. "And I'm gonna turn up the heat in our search for Marco Meriwether. Maybe that female from the projects he allegedly put in a coma has woken up."

Kenya

Storm put his key in the door and stepped inside the condo to find his brother in the kitchen dancing to the sounds of the stereo as he made himself at home cooking. Knowing that O.T. hadn't heard him come in, he crept up behind him. "What up, buster?" He smiled. "What it do, playa?"

O.T. spun around pulling his gun out his waistband thrown off his square. "Damn, nigga! You almost made me put some of this fire to ya ass!" He let his guard back down. "You better announce yourself next time!"

"The day I gotta announce myself in my own fucking house is the day you'll see me in a dress and nine-inch heels!" Storm was amused heading to the refrigerator to get a glass of juice. "And what the fuck is you in here burning anyhow? It smells like old mop water!"

O.T. turned his attention back to the stove adding some seasoning salt to the pot he had simmering. "I was making some soup for me and London. She's upstairs lying down in her old room."

"Dig that." Storm scratched his beard then downed the rest of his juice as he fished for information not trying to seem jealous and territorial as O.T. had recently accused him of being. "Did you put your stuff in the basement?"

"Naw, nigga! It's up in London's room." O.T. chuckled. "Why?"

"What?" Storm coughed almost choking.

"I'm just bullshittin', dawg! Don't kill me!" O.T. threw up his hands enjoying the expression on his brother's face.

"Fuck you, nigga!"

O.T. stirred the pot of soup then dipped a small amount of it out to taste. "Dang, I almost forgot. Where is Queen Kenya?" He blew onto the spoon.

"I left her still sitting out in the car mad as five runaway slaves who just got caught one block away from freedom."

"Whoa." O.T. swallowed the hot soup. "How long she gonna play the victim role? No bullshittin', I know she should be pissed the fuck off, but damn! It ain't like her sister want you! London don't even say your name!"

Even though that wasn't his girl, Storm still had a hard time dealing with the realism of the fact the mother of his child couldn't care less if he lived or died. He realized over the past few months before he knew she was pregnant he'd treated her poorly, but he hoped for the baby's sake she had forgiven him. Now, to let his little brother tell it, she didn't even want the child to know he was the biological father. At this point he felt like nothing more than a sperm donor at best. He always wanted to be a father; now not only was his girl bugging behind the bizarre circumstances, so was her twin.

"I don't know why Kenya is still tripping." Storm moved the blinds just in time to hear the engine start and his girl back the car out the driveway.

"Dang, where she going to now?" O.T. questioned on his way up the stairs with a bowl of soup for London.

"We gotta do something to bring these two back together."

"Real talk, especially since we gonna be housing with each other, but shit Kenya so crazy right about now I don't know what it could be."

"Whatever the fuck it is, we better come up with it quick!" O.T. shrugged his shoulders.

Noticing the one bar he had left, Storm sat in his favorite chair by the lamp plugging his cell phone into the electric outlet so it could get fully charged. Picking up the house phone reluctant for another argument, he forced himself to call Kenya. By the time he'd dialed the last digit of her number he'd kicked his shoes off and was making himself comfortable.

"Yes," Kenya answered with a dry tone.

"Where is you going?"

"Why you care?" She didn't raise her voice. "Don't you have your precious London and y'all son all up in your house?"

"First off, Kenya, this is our house."

"Nigga, please! I sure can't tell!" She turned the corner jumping down on the freeway. "'Cause if it was any part of my house, her fat ass wouldn't ever step foot inside it again! But since she is in there despite my wishes that just about says it all!"

"Yeah, all right, can you at least tell me when you plan on bringing my damn car back?"

"When the fuck I get ready, that's when!"

"Kenya, stop acting like you ain't got no sense and bring my shit back. I got business to take care of later! Plus it's not safe out in them streets!"

"Boy, bye! You ain't my damn daddy!" she dismissed him as she pressed down on the gas pedal, flipped her cell closed, tossing it onto the passenger seat, and turned the radio volume up.

Hearing one sad-ass love song after the next, a depressed Kenya came up on the exit for Paris's apartment. Driving around to the rear entrance, Kenya parked Storm's car on the far side of the lot near the black iron gates that surrounded the swimming pool. Popping the trunk she got her bag out and carried it in. When she got to the door she fumbled through her purse looking for the keys. *Dang, I gotta clean this messy thang up.* Finding the red rabbit foot keychain

Kenya unlocked the first of three deadbolts, when she thought she heard someone in the stairwell. "Hello, hello?" she paused. "Is anyone there?"

Not getting a response, Kenya assumed she was just hearing things and opened the remaining locks going inside the empty apartment. Things hadn't changed much since the last time she was there a few months ago. The same now mold-infested filthy dishes, messy living room, and unmade bed were staring her in the face. Grabbing a huge garbage bag from underneath the sink, Kenya gathered all the cups, saucers, bowls, pots, and pans, throwing them inside, tightly tying the bag. After filling two more, smaller bags, she dragged them all to the front door leaving them there to be thrown out in the Dumpster when she left.

Changing the sheets in the guest bedroom and thoroughly scrubbing and disinfecting the bathroom, Kenya opened her small suitcase making herself at home. Running a hot bubble bath, she stripped down and was about to put one foot in the tub when the buzzer rang.

That's probably Storm chasing behind me, she figured as it rang twice more. *I don't even know why he here.* Kenya wrapped a towel around her nude body making her way down the hall and to the intercom. "Who is it?" No one answered her so she asked once more this time louder. "Yeah, who is it?"

Still standing in the living room she heard something hit one of the windows. Spinning around, she clutched her towel and suspiciously tip-toed in that direction. As she stood on the side of the wall she heard the noise again. Rattled with fear, she hesitantly peeped out the dark beige curtain seeing nothing but a car with a broken taillight and the muffler hanging roar out of the lot.

Ring. Ring. Ring. Startled by the sound of her cell phone Kenya dropped the towel to the carpet. Bending over picking it back up to cover herself, she ran to her purse flipping her Razor open before even seeing who the caller was. "Hello?"

"Where you at? I'm tired of playing all these games with you!"

"Storm, is that you?" Kenya's eyes quickly searched the room from the spot she was standing in as she got a bad migraine. "Was you just pushing the buzzer?"

"Naw, what is you talking about? What buzzer? Where in the fuck is you?"

"Somebody was ringing Paris's doorbell and throwing something at the window." She started to calm down as she spoke. "Maybe they just had the wrong apartment."

"Listen, Kenya," he urged. "Make sure all the doors are locked and just sit tight. I'm about to get your car out the garage and be on my way over there."

Kenya was paranoid and did exactly as she was told.

Storm, not wasting another moment, put his shoes back on, grabbed his pistol out a shoebox in the front closet, and yelled upstairs to his brother who was still preoccupied with catering to London. "Yo! I'll be back! I think ol' boy was out by your spot just now!" He sounded drastic as he rushed to retrieve Kenya's spare keys out the junk drawer in the kitchen.

"What! That punk Marco?" O.T. ran to the edge of the top stair just as Storm was on his way out. "Wait up, my dude, I'm going with you!"

"Naw, I'm good. Do ya thang!" Storm hissed seeing his brother shirtless revealing his over twenty tattoos. "I holler if I need you."

Marco

I knew sooner or damn later one of them assholes would show up, Marco vengefully thought as he placed a note on Storm's car that was parked in Paris's lot.

These niggas think I'm gonna go from making thousands a week to starving and that's it! Payback is a mother!

Hitting every side street he could to avoid contact with the police, Marco drove to a secluded part of a bank parking lot and waited for the perfect person to arrive. With no more than ten minutes passing, a car pulled up with what appeared to be several young children along with a middle-aged woman driver. Having committed this ruthless crime before, Marco was always wise enough to pick a bank that had no drive-through accessibility, only a walkup ATM machine, forcing the person to get out the security of their automobile.

Knowing there was a bounty on his head made him more valuable than a new pair of exclusive Jordans two weeks before the release date. Things were most definitely hard, as his homeboy Coonee pointed out time and time again to Marco every day he chose to crash at his spot. This night he wasn't in the mood to hear that speech and decided to bless his boy along with himself with some much-needed cash.

"I'll be right back, so just sit still," the lady yelled out to her children as she approached the machine with purse in hand.

Marco reached in the rear seat of his raggedy car getting a royal blue hoodie, throwing it on. Checking first to see if the coast was clear, he made his move. Seeing the pudgy-shaped female was preoccupied searching for her card, he put on his hood tucking most of his dreads in and crept up behind her. "Bitch, check that shit in!"

"Oh my God! Please! Please!" she begged as tears instantly started to flow feeling a huge gun pressed in her rib cage. "Don't hurt us!"

"That all depends on you. Now shut the fuck up and put that card in there!" Marco demanded glancing back at the kids who were busy arguing with one another about a movie they'd just come back from.

"Okay, but please don't hurt me and my kids."

"Didn't I say shut the fuck up? Don't keep playing with me!" He shoved the barrel hard proving that he wasn't messing around with her and meant business. "If ya keep running that fat-ass mouth of yours instead of getting my motherfucking dough, me and you gonna have a serious misunderstanding real quick and your kids gonna be missing they momma! Ya feel me?"

"Yes, yes." She spoke under her breath as she pushed in her pin number, taking out $300 and handing it to Marco.

"That's it?" He snatched it out her trembling hands counting the amount. "Get me some more!"

"I can't!" The woman began to sob noticing her children were getting restless in the car. "It won't let me. That's my daily limit."

"You broke bitch!" Marco stuck his gun back in the front pocket of his hoodie to conceal it when another car drove by. As he turned around to head back to his vehicle he saw the woman take a picture of him out the corner of his eye with her cell phone. "What did you just do?"

"Nothing," she stuttered. "I didn't do anything!"

Marco, callously not giving a shit what the kids were about to witness, snatched the phone from their mother's hands and let two rounds go striking her in the stomach. Running back to his car he drove away quickly leaving her sprawled out in front of the bank with her kids gathered around crying. Coming to a dark street, Marco yanked the hoodie off throwing it out the window and headed over to Coonee's crib where tonight they would eat and smoke like kings.

Kenya

Climbing the stairs two at a time, Storm stood outside Paris's door banging until Kenya opened it up looking like she'd seen a ghost. "Storm!"

"Yeah, you good or what?" He pushed passed her with his burner out ready to lay a Negro seriously down for the count. "Did anything else jump?"

"Naw, I haven't moved from the other room until now."

"Listen, you gotta stop doing all this dumb shit! You gonna mess around and get everybody killed or arrested one." Storm led her over to the couch insisting she sit down. "Now, for real I'm done playing these silly immature head games with you. Either you can accept the bullshit that's going on or you can pack all your junk, not just a suitcase, but all your stuff and go back home to Detroit. If you don't wanna go back there I'll get you a place wherever you wanna go, but this situation I've been going through this past year is ridiculous," he lectured with a look of frustration as he paced the small room. "I know I done told some lies, but I just didn't wanna hurt you anymore. So if you choose to bounce, then do it because I'm tired as hell trying to please all y'all motherfuckers!"

Kenya was at a loss for words. Storm, once the man of her dreams, was issuing her an ultimatum to either stand by him or stand alone. She could tell that this was it and her pity party had come to an abrupt end. They'd gone back and forth about this and that for months and now it had come down to this very moment in her best friend's house on her best friend's couch. Kenya's destiny was about to be decided by the next words she spoke.

Taking a deep breath after considering what was at stake, she told Storm what was on her mind. "Do I love you? Hell yeah, I do! Can I get over the fact you and my sister having a baby? Maybe I can and maybe I can't, but the one thing I can't and won't get over is being lied to all the time!" She paused to gather her thoughts. "Right here, right now if you tell me everything that got to do with you and that baby, I'll believe you and we can try to move on from here, but if I find out anymore sneaky shit, I'm done and I will go back to Detroit!"

"You already know all there is to know, plus it seems like my brother gonna end up being my child's father anyhow."

"Well, I don't know what that means." Kenya got up standing toe-to-toe with him. "But if you care anything about me you won't lie anymore about jack shit!"

Storm reassured her of his commitment to their once tranquil relationship and swore the secret keeping was over. Anything he did concerning London and the baby, he'd run by Kenya first. Still in a towel Kenya ran another tubful of water and seductively stepped in. Storm sat on the edge watching Kenya bathe as long as he could before undressing, getting in himself.

Chapter 13

Hard Times

Police

"We just got a call from one of the officers who's on the stakeout." Malloy hung up the office phone with a smile of contentment. "It seems they ran the plate on a car that is registered to Tony Christian parked out in the Shady Tree Estates lot."

"That's good business." Kendrick clenched his fist. "If he's over there his brother can't be far behind."

"Yeah, I told the guys to keep a close watch, but from afar."

"That was quick. What time did they pick up the hit?"

"They got in position about three this morning and that's when they first spotted the vehicle."

Hopeful that soon it would be some sort of a break in the open cases, the partners went to grab a quick breakfast from an out of the way down-home cooking hole in the wall. Calling ahead placing their food order gave the two detectives time to hang up some more posters pertaining to the capture of their number one suspect in a long list of crimes, including one extremely high-priority complaint that came in just hours earlier in which a single mother of four was robbed and killed in front of her children. The eldest child, just ten years old, described through his tears and grief Marco Meriwether as the lone gunman. With the reward money being increased to $15,000 in light of the latest homicide, maybe someone from the crime-infested community would step up and turn him in.

"Number 103, your order is ready." The cashier rang up the two breakfasts placing them in a white plastic bag for the officers who headed toward the exit dropping off some flyers on the bench. "Number 104, you up!" she then yelled out.

Bumping into the young guy who was getting up to pay for his food, Kendrick politely excused himself. When Coonee made sure the detectives had pulled out the gravel-filled lot, he picked up one of the flyers that had his homeboy's picture on it. REWARD OF $15,000 was all the broke, out-of-product street soldier could pay attention to. Folding the paper up, he put it in his back pocket then gave the cashier a crisp twenty dollar bill Marco had given him the night before, which was obviously blood money, got the food, and left.

An eviction notice, an empty-ass refrigerator, new sneakers, and his car fixed was all Coonee kept thinking about on the way back to his apartment with his and Marco's breakfast. *Fifteen thousand motherfucking dollars!*

O.T.

"How was your first night back in your old room?" O.T. asked London as she came down the stairs looking for any signs of her twin.

"I hardly slept." She yawned. "I guess I was busy sleeping with one eye open just in case Kenya was thinking about stabbing me or something."

"Storm called last night and said him and your sister were gonna stay at my apartment and would be back this morning." O.T. didn't want to upset her by letting her know that Storm believed Marco was lurking around and Kenya might've been in danger.

"Oh, okay." London felt relieved she could fix herself a bit of breakfast and wash dishes without looking over her shoulder in fear of Kenya's harsh, judgmental words.

Ring. Ring. Ring. O.T. took the cordless phone off the charger and read the word UNAVAILABLE on the caller ID. "Yeah, hello."

"You have a collect call from Tangy. Will you accept the charges?"

"Hell naw!" O.T. rudely laughed into the operator's ear before hanging up. Thirty seconds later, the phone rang again. When he picked it up he heard the same speech, this time from a different operator.

"You have a collect call from Tangy. Will you accept the charges, sir?"

Knowing the lunatic broad was gonna keep trying to get through all morning O.T. agreed. "Yeah, I will."

"Caller, go ahead."

"Hello?" Tangy said.

"What's up, dumb bitch?"

"Who in the fuck is this?"

"Who it sound like, with ya dyke tramp self!"

"O.T. is this your stupid-ass?"

"You still tough as a motherfucker even locked behind those bars. I was just telling our girl Vanessa that the other night when me and her had dinner."

"Fuck you, nigga! It ain't over between me and Vanessa! I owe that bitch one just like I owe ya punk-ass! Now where is Kenya? Put her on the line!"

"Girl, my sister-in-law ain't thinking about you, so stop dialing this number trying to call shots, you fucking cell gangster!" O.T. teased. "What is you trying to do anyway, steal my brother's woman and turn her out?"

"O.T., you ain't shit!" Tangy screamed through the phone once more. "I hate your ass!"

"Whatever you say, just talk quick 'cause you on my dime."

"Well, have you went to visit my little cousin?"

"Naw, what in the hell do I need to see that crazy bitch for?" O.T. made sure London, who was still in the kitchen, could hear him. "Me and Paris is through! That's a wrap and if that cuckoo for Cocoa Puffs chick ever talks again she'll tell you that shit her damn self!"

"O.T., you ain't about nothing! One day ya luck gonna run out! Trust that! You just can't keep running over people and think that payback ain't gonna come back on your dumb-ass! Karma is a motherfucker!"

"I know, I know. And I wanna thank you for all the compliments not to mention all your great, wise, and powerful words of wisdom, oh great pussy eater on lockdown, and FYI, ya time is up!" O.T. clicked the phone off with a smile on his face.

Storm

After a long, hot night of back-to-back banging, Storm and Kenya left Paris's apartment with a brand new attitude on life. There would be no more blatant lies or misconceptions on what either of them were doing. With a lot of things on both their agendas, Kenya turned left on the highway and Storm made a right as his cell phone rang.

"Hey, O.T."

"What up, bro, any more signs of that faggot Marco?"

"Naw, he ain't show back up, but he left a note on my damn windshield."

"What that garbage say?"

"It was a bad drawing of a gun that said bang ya dead!"

"Who that guy think he is, Clint Eastwood and shit!"

"Yeah, right, but that guy don't really want none!" Storm checked his watch. "But it just let us know we gotta find his ass."

"Don't worry, after this morning, Marco gonna be ghost 'cause now I'm gonna hunt him!"

"Well, I just have to swing by Alley Cats and meet with a couple of contractors, the plumber, and a few electricians who are gonna give me their bids."

"Then what?" O.T. asked his brother as he went upstairs to get dressed.

"And then I'll be back out to the condo."

"All right then, I'll holler at you later. I'm about to go down to the projects and see if any of them dudes heard shit about where Marco been laying his head."

"Watch ya back! Peace."

Police

"What should we do?" the officer debated with his relief who had just arrived. "Do we follow him or her?"

"Our orders are to watch Tony Christian from afar not his girl."

"All right then, have a good day and I'll call you with my location about four o'clock."

As the plainclothes undercover officer started his shift on the round-the-clock surveillance, Storm's car drove by causing him to duck down or risk being seen. With enough safe distance between them, he then took off following Storm's every move.

Kenya

"Hey now, Charday, please tell a sista you can try to fit me in?" Kenya called her stylist hoping she could get her hair done at the last minute. Taking a quick glance up in the rearview mirror she could see she was looking a hot freaking mess. After all the times and different positions she and Storm had sexually partaken in last night she needed to get herself together.

"Wait a minute, let me check with Sable." Charday had the receptionist do a quick rundown of her schedule to find any late cancellations. If there was any way possible to hook up a good tipping customer she was definitely going to try.

"Please, girl, I need you! Otherwise I'm gonna have to go to the damn beauty supply and buy a wig!"

"Yeah, Kenya, I can squeeze you in but you gotta hurry okay?" She laughed at Kenya's last comment. "So come on."

"Not a problem, chick. I'm on my way!"

Just as promised Kenya pushed the accelerator and arrived at Hair In Da Hood in record time. Not wasting a moment by gossiping like she always did when she came in for her appointment, Kenya immediately went to get shampooed. Lying back in the chair as the girl let the warm water rinse through her hair, she got one of her super painful and intense headaches that she'd been suffering from the past few weeks.

Dizzy, feeling nauseated as she got her hair blown dry and styled, Kenya thought she was going to pass out right there on the spot in the beauty shop chair.

"Are you okay?" Charday whispered tapping her client lightly on the shoulder. "You look like hot fired death on a stick."

"Girl, I don't know what's wrong with me, just stress I guess. I've been trying to deal with them funny-acting insurance claim adjusters and you know I just came back from Detroit visiting my people."

"Yeah, well you better go home and rest your nerves for a while," Charday urged as she took the cape off Kenya and walked her to the door.

At the same time she was trying to leave, Vanessa and some bitch were coming in. With an aqua-colored scarf wrapped tightly around her head, Vanessa mean mugged Kenya as she used her shoulder to bump her as the two passed one another.

"Excuse you!" Vanessa kept her hand in her purse on her blade knowing from witnessing firsthand that Kenya was no joke and could buck with the best of them.

"Watch where you going!" Kenya was sick, but still wasn't gonna get punked at the salon.

"Or what you gonna do? Get Tangy to kick my ass?"

"Look, honey." Kenya cracked a slight smile. "Please believe me when I tell you don't nobody want Tangy's crazy tripped-out ass but you! So why don't you do your pitiful self a huge favor and go on inside and get your wig fixed before I lose my patience and end up splitting that motherfucker!"

"Come on now, Vanessa. I don't know why every time you come in my salon you try to start something about that damned whorish Tangy." Charday put her two cents in setting the record straight. "You know as well as every other bitch in Dallas knows Tangy be flirting with every female she comes in contact with! So calm the hell down and stop fucking with my customers!"

Vanessa's friend pulled her arm yanking her inside the salon for their appointments, knowing that Kenya and Charday were both right and she was making a spectacle out of herself.

"All right then, chick. Go on home and take care of yourself and call me if you need to."

"Thanks, girl." Kenya hugged Charday before practically dragging herself in the car and finally heading home to find God knows what.

Chapter 14

Double Take

Storm

Sitting in his car riffling through the mountains of paperwork the various contractors had bombarded him with, Storm knew the renovation of Alley Cats was gonna cost him a small fortune. With an ongoing arson investigation holding up the insurance check, the drought that was crippling his drug revenue, and now a baby on the way, financially things were getting out of hand.

Placing both hands over his face trying to figure out some sort of temporary solutions to his complicated, twisted dilemmas, like a gift from God, his cell phone rang.

"Yeah, hello."

"As-Salaam Alaikum."

"Greetings, Brother Rasul," Storm respectfully replied. "I'm glad you called so soon. To be honest with you I'm at the end of my rope with my resources."

"Not to worry, Storm, everything is in place. Fatima is still agitated as hell for me doing it, but Kenya and I go far back and our friendship doesn't have boundaries or restrictions on it."

"I appreciate all the love, devotion, and respect you have for my girl."

"Not a problem, Storm, but on the other hand you need to know that you and you alone are a hundred percent responsible for the ticket on that package and will be held totally accountable for payment in no more than thirty days," Brother Rasul strongly advised.

"I hear you. Thirty days." Storm was elated that very soon his street soldiers would be back on the grind and money would once again start flowing freely.

"Storm, listen to me. If something does go wrong, I can't and won't intervene. Not even for Kenya's sake. Do we have a complete understanding of our deal?"

"You have my word that your people will have their money in thirty days."

"One last thing is that you must be on time because you only have once to make a good first impression with these people. Any foul-ups or discrepancies, you can trust you'll never get a second chance dealing with them ever again."

"Don't worry, Brother Rasul, I won't mess up!"

With that exchange understood, Brother Rasul gave Storm the contact information along with the precise time and location of the drop, which, for safety precautions, he kept locked in his memory instead of writing it down. Having just received a new lease on life Storm turned out of the parking lot of his temporarily closed strip club and started on his way home. After several red lights and three left turns, he soon came to suspect he was being followed. By who, he didn't know for sure. But whoever it was he knew they should buckle their seat belts and hold the fuck on.

Reaching under the driver seat Storm took out his pistol, setting it on his lap just in case, then checked his mirrors. Slowly approaching the next intersection, he acted as if he was going to stop, then gunned it through the yellow light, made a quick left, then flew up a back alleyway and finally recklessly hooked a U-turn on the next major street four blocks over. *If a mother-fucker can follow all of that, he need to catch my black-ass!* Storm thought as he drove around the outskirts of the city twenty more minutes before jumping on the highway heading toward his condo. *It doesn't matter if that was Marco or the cops; fuck 'em both!*

Reunions . . .

"Wow, I should have never let O.T. cook for me last night. He must have used every dish and pot Kenya owns." London giggled as she looked under the sink for more soap and a Brillo Pad.

Barely able to bend down and reach the box near the corner, she struggled to get back up when she heard the front door slam shut. Thinking it was her sister, London turned to shamefully creep back upstairs and out of Kenya's way. Before she could get out the kitchen, she was met by Storm.

"Oh hey, it's you."

"Yeah, who was you expecting, O.T.?"

"No, he just left. I thought you were Kenya and I didn't want to be in her path."

"Oh, you mean the Big Bad Wolf, huh?" Storm tried to ease the tension that had been a constant barrier between him and London for months.

"You shouldn't play like that. I know how she must feel and it's awful." London grabbed her stomach and took a deep breath.

"What's wrong with you?" Storm got close holding her up by her arm. "Are you okay?"

"It's nothing." London moved away remembering what happened the last time they were in the house alone in the kitchen. "The baby just kicked."

"Damn!" Storm smiled. "You're lying! Let me feel him."

"Okay." She was slightly hesitant placing his hand on her left side. "Just wait a second."

"Oh, shit! I just felt him! He gonna be strong, I can tell!"

London lowered her head walking into the living room sitting down on the couch. "I hope so."

"What's that supposed to mean?" He followed concerned for his unborn son. "What's wrong with my baby?"

"It's just you and O.T. tip-toe around me trying to act like everything is okay and it isn't. I know that crazy guy from the mall is the same one who murdered your friend Boz and now he's promising to kill you and O.T.!"

"Yeah, you're right," he admitted.

London shed a few tears trying to still remain brave. "Well, if something happens to either one of you, my child is going to suffer a major loss not being able to grow up with his father or his uncle in his life. And the way things stand with Kenya he won't have his aunt."

Storm was now faced with the brutal reality that London was right. The life he and O.T. were living was a death sentence waiting to occur, but he was too far in the game, with too much responsibility on his plate to back out now and call it quits. There was only one thing he could do to protect his son's interest in the long run and that would be on the top of his to-do list.

As the two of them sat talking, he tried convincing London that Kenya had accepted the fact that he wanted to be a part of the baby's life and was going to at least be civil to her. Before Storm and she knew it, Kenya had put her key in the front door and was coming inside. Waiting nervously they braced themselves for a huge blowout when she saw both of them together interacting. Shockingly something was drastically wrong. It had to be, because the pair got a surprise of a lifetime. A disoriented Kenya hardly looked their way and quietly went up the stairs shutting her bedroom door.

"Why is she looking like that?" London wanted to come to her twin sister's aid, but was stopped by Storm.

"Naw, you stay down here. I got her."

"Okay," London sadly replied.

Chapter 15

With Friends Like These

Kenya

It had been a long, emotionally charged night. Kenya tossed and turned not sleeping more than twenty to thirty minutes at a time. Suffering excruciating abdominal pains, any food that was in her stomach was totally out of her system thanks to intense bouts of vomiting. After constant refusals from Kenya to go seek medical attention, Storm finally stepped in making the decision for her.

"You not getting any better, so fuck all the dumb shit I'm taking ya ass to the hospital!"

Assisting his woman put on a pair of track pants and one of his T-shirts, Storm swooped her in his arms carrying her weak body down the stairs and out to his car not bothering to notice he was being watched.

"Call me and tell me something!" Helplessly, London stood outside her bedroom door wanting nothing more than to be there by Kenya's side as she was being taken out. Rubbing her ever-growing belly, London cringed as she now had one more thing to worry about. First O.T. hadn't come home at all last night and now Kenya was sick.

O.T.

Being persistent on his hunt for Marco was proving to be a dangerous mission. Fed up with all the hide and seek games Marco was playing, O.T. brazenly hung out in the places his prey was known to frequent hoping word would get back to him that O.T. was calling him out. Yet no one in the pool halls, corner stores, or afterhours spots seemed to know anything about Marco's whereabouts and O.T. was done with the chase until nightfall.

Exhausted from roaming the coldblooded project streets keeping his ear pressed to the ground, O.T. decided to shoot out to the condo, take a shower, and grab some food. So, wasting no time he drove to his brother's house. As he turned into the driveway and parked he heard his cell phone ring.

"Yeah, what it do?"

"Hey, O.T., it's me."

"Wow, you must've missed me or something."

"Well, I was worried a little bit," London admitted as she sighed with relief her child's uncle wasn't hurt or dead. "But, the real reason I called was to tell you that Storm had to rush my sister to the hospital."

"Dang, don't tell me she pulled a Paris?" He laughed, jumping out the car walking to the front door.

"Don't act stupid!"

"I was just playing." He surprised London by coming in the room she was sitting at. "What happened?"

Both of them hung up their phones and smiled.

"Why you play so much?"

"Sorry." He hugged her. "Now tell me what exactly happened."

London explained all the details as O.T. stuffed his face with leftovers. She also told him what she and Storm had spoken about the afternoon before. O.T. tried to act as if he didn't care about their heart-to-heart conversation, but of course he was hurt. The hardcore criminal for the first time in his life wanted something that he couldn't steal, or strong-arm or manipulate the system to achieve. And that was London's

love. If O.T. took the time to really step back and
see the whole picture for what it truly was
he'd see he already had that.

"I just wish Kenya would forgive me. I want
my sister back in my life. How can she accept
Storm and not me?"

Marco

"I done stayed posted up in this motherfucker
all yesterday and trust a nigga like me getting
beyond bored as hell." Marco stretched his arms
rubbing the crusty sleep out the corner of his
eyes. "I need to get some real bread in my hands,
settle my beef, and kill them two wannabe gang-
sta brothers and get out of dodge!"

"I feel ya, Marco, but you know them streets
is hot with the cops. Plus when I was at the store
last night grabbing them forties, I seen O.T.
lurking around," Coonee cautiously warned his
boy as he peeped out the front window. "Shit, he
damn near fucked around and bumped into me."

"What! Why ain't you say that shit before?"
Marco leaped to his feet enraged. "That ho-ass
motherfucker down here in our neck of the
woods and you didn't let that bitch have it?"

"Huh?" Coonee was puzzled. "What you
mean?"

"Are you retarded or something?" Marco pounded his fist. "You heard me!"

Coonee, who was at least four years Marco's junior, was thrown off at his boy's irate reaction, who knew full well ever since the night Royce and their two boys had gotten killed, Coonee had shied away from the street life and all the elements that went along with it and was looking for a nine-to-five job. Yet when Marco unexpectedly showed up drunk and disorderly at his front door needing somewhere to chill, Coonee, who could easily get charged with harboring a fugitive, didn't think twice about letting him hide out.

"What did you want me to do? Kill that man in the store where everybody could see?"

"Hell yeah, I did!" Marco yelled back getting all up in Coonee's face. "You was talking all that shit the other day about killing Storm's pregnant bitch in the mall, now you standing here acting a straight pussy!"

Wiping small amounts of spit off his face, Coonee was heated. "Hold up, nigga! This ya thang ya got going on with them dudes! I know that shit was fucked up the night Royce got killed, but you did start it by ambushing them innocent workers from Alley Cats."

"So fucking what! It's all part of the game, you must of all of a sudden, be too weak to play!"

"Listen, Marco, you's my boy and all, but you know I'm trying to do something different." Coonee thought back to the night he was staring down the barrel of O.T.'s gun who gave him a second chance on life. "I ain't trying to get locked up or killed."

Marco was starting to get the picture and realized it was time for him and Coonee to sever their dealings.

"I'll tell you what. Why don't I just stay here a couple of more nights then I'll be out your hair." Marco calmed down as he started to scheme on a final game plan for revenge. "'Cause I can see you and me cut from different cloths."

"Don't worry about it, guy!" Coonee let his guard down trusting in the friendship the two once shared. "Do what you need to do. Ya know you can stay as long as you need to! I'm gonna jump in the shower 'cause I got a job interview and I don't wanna be late."

"A job interview?" Marco laughed falling back on the worn, torn couch. "You is out ya shit!"

Coonee, who was filthy, took off the blue jeans he'd been wearing for three days straight tossing them in the enormous pile of dirty clothes that were starting to smell. While the thundering sounds of the steaming hot water came down on him, he heard Marco call out his name.

"Coonee! Hey, nigga! You got my lighter?"

"Dang, my bad!" Coonee stuck his head out the shower yelling back. "I think it's in my pocket."

"All right then I'll check." Marco, with his unlit blunt hanging in between his lips, went over to the pile grabbing Coonee's jeans off the top. Shaking them upside down, his blue lighter fell out onto the floor along with a folded-up sheet of paper. Being nosey he opened it. *Ain't this a bitch! This ho-ass motherfucker running around here acting like he against slinging dope and killing some busters who got it coming, when all along he plotting to turn me the fuck in to get this damn reward money!* Marco crumpled the flyer, which his picture graced, throwing it against the wall. *No wonder he want me to stick around a few more days. He ain't got no job interview. That snitch probably going to meet up with the police!*

Smoking his blunt, Marco waited patiently for Coonee to get out the shower and get dressed. As the aroma filled the air, his hands began to itch. Leering at his soon-to-be victim as he looked for his social security card and birth certificate, Marco's heart rate increased. "How you getting to this interview of yours?"

"I'm getting a ride from this chick I met last night."

"Oh, yeah?" Marco put the blunt in the ashtray. "You ain't tell me you met a new hood rat."

"Oh, I must've forgot!" Coonee grinned. "She's a bad bitch, too! When I get my car fixed, I'm gonna take her out to the park or some romantic shit like that!"

"You forgetting a lot of stuff all of a sudden and damn, you must be expecting a windfall, talking about getting ya ride fixed and caking with a tramp!" Marco angrily probed as he sat his gun on the coffee table.

"What is you trying to say, dawg?

"You know what it is, ya snitch!"

"What the hell is you talking about?" Coonee started to sweat wondering where Marco's irrational brain was at calling him a snitch. "I ain't try to do nothing, but tolerate your off-the-chart-ass!"

"You think I don't know where you really going and what you 'bout to do?"

Coonee, dressed in dark navy blue slacks, white shirt, and a cornball SpongeBob necktie in his hands, was truly bewildered and confused as to what direction his boy was coming from. "Damn, dude, you need to leave them trees the hell alone 'cause you tripping." He started putting his tie on. "You need some professional help!"

Before Coonee could get a chance to hear any kind of a response, Marco unexpectedly jumped to his feet lunging at him resulting in the two of them falling into the stereo system that was on an already wobbly shelf. With his temper in overdrive Marco yanked hard on his tie swiftly wrapping it around his arms using his overpowering strength to strangle Coonee down to his knees. As the two men violently struggled, an almost out of breath Coonee who was fighting for his life finally broke free from Marco's grip and got up stumbling to the other side of the room.

Marco, unfortunately for Coonee, wasn't done with his sinister tirade and showed no outward signs of sympathy for his homeboy or his ripped shirt. "Why don't you go out and do some grown-man shit instead of being a ho-ass snitch to get some loot?" he continued to talk tough. "Niggas like me out here every single day getting that shit in, putting in work, and you running around like a little rat!"

"What the fuck is wrong with you?" Coonee held his neck panting for air. "Why you doing this?"

"Shut ya soft-ass up!" Marco ranted fueled with a passion. "You think I'm gonna just sit around and wait for you and them motherfuckers to hem me up?" He cracked his knuckles rushing Coonee once more, this time bulldozing him underneath his ribs lifting him off the ground.

Ramming Coonee into the thin plastered walls, huge pieces of chipped paint fell to the ground. Only having a thin pair of dress socks on, the tiny, sharp broken edges cut Coonee's feet. With a slight weight advantage Marco used to his benefit, he took both his fists and slammed the sides of Coonee's temples at the same time. Seeing his now ex-friend's injured body hit the ground, Marco capitalized on the situation, grabbing a Phillips-head screwdriver from under the television stand jabbing it in Coonee's side puncturing one of his lungs.

Getting pleasure watching him suffer in agony and Coonee's once white interview shirt become soaked with blood, Marco pulled the screwdriver out and stuck his victim again, this time in the middle of his chest twisting it around. *Oh it ain't over yet, you snitchin'-ass faggot!* As he stood up feeling almost satisfied with himself, in one last act to make him feel totally victorious, Marco raised his sneaker stumping Coonee directly in his stomach rupturing more vital organs.

"So, you was gonna turn me the fuck in to the popo, huh?" Marco spewed as slobber came out the left corner of his mouth seeing Coonee meet his Maker. "I always knew you wasn't shit!"

Lying back getting relaxed and comfortable on the couch, Marco kicked his feet up on the coffee table using the blue lighter reblazing his blunt while staring at his homeboy's dead body. After a hour of getting good, faded, and high as a son of a bitch, Marco disrespectfully dragged Coonee to the far corner of his bedroom gathering the huge pile of dirty smelly clothes throwing them on top of him so you could only see the bottom of Coonee's socks.

Police

"Hey, Malloy, I'm still on Storm's trail. It looks like he just carried his girlfriend through emergency."

"Okay, stay with him," Malloy radioed back to the undercover officer. "It seems like his brother O.T. spent the night trying to do our job for us."

"Oh, yeah? How so?"

"Yeah, I just got the word that he was in the projects trying to track down Marco Meriwether," Malloy further informed him. "That lets me know we definitely on the right track on who is to blame for those four homicides."

Chapter 16

Harsh Reality

Storm

As Storm posted up in the hospital waiting room he sat back thinking how his life had drastically changed, some things bad and a few things for the better. Even though he knew all the controversy the birth of his son was going to cause that was still his flesh and blood. He heard London's valid concerns for him and his brother's lifestyle ring in his ears repeatedly and reached on his hip for his cell phone.

"Good afternoon. Law offices of Jeffery Benson and Associates, how can I help you?"

"Hey there, Yolanda, is Jeff in yet?"

Recognizing one of their favorite and frequent clients' voices, Yolanda had smiled as she answered. "Yes, sir, Mr. Christian, he just got in from court. Would you like to hold?"

"Yeah, I'll hold." Storm leaned back as he waited.

"Hey, Storm! My main man!"

"What it do, Jeff?" he quizzed not really giving a fuck.

"Just getting back from plea bargining some knucklehead probation, but that's neither here nor there. What can I do for you?"

"I need you to set up a trust fund or some shit like that for a baby just in case something happens to me."

"A baby? Don't tell me congratulations are in order for you and Kenya! When's the due date?"

Storm, although ashamed of his actions had to come clean with his lawyer, who on more than several occasions he'd trusted with his life and freedom. "Well, Jeff, it's like this . . ."

"Are you serious?" Attorney Jeffery Benson inquired having been told a heap of crazy stories throughout the duration of his long career. "Whoa twins? And you didn't know the difference?"

"Can you help me? Those papers would make life easier for me to make moves without second-guessing my shit."

After explaining the bizarre made-for-television story, Jeff promised by noon the next day Storm could stop by, sign, have notarized, and pick up all the documents he needed to ensure the child's financial security. Handling that business was a gigantic burden off his shoulders and would hopefully be one off of London's also. Now, he could get back to worrying about Kenya and, of course, that parasite Marco.

Kenya

After hours of Storm sitting and sleeping in the waiting room Kenya was escorted out by the nurse having a look of disorientation, disappointment, and regret. The fresh hairdo Charday had given her the day before was wrecked and Kenya's eyes were red and puffy.

"Hey, babe." Storm stood up reaching out for her shaking hands. "Are you okay? I asked them bitches at the desk four times if I could come back there with you, but they kept saying you was taking different tests and shit."

"Let's just go home," Kenya barely whispered holding on to his arm with one hand while grasping a group of papers that included releases, prescriptions, and a few pamphlets. "I just wanna leave."

"Come on, babe!" Storm was persistent as they left out the sliding double doors. "I been out here all this time and you ain't gonna tell me what's the deal? Damn, what did the doctor say was wrong with you?"

"I'll tell you later. Please, just take me home!"

"Say you promise!" Storm kissed her on the forehead using her favorite saying.

"Yeah, baby, I promise!" Kenya rubbed her arms getting a slight chill from the evening air as he opened her car door helping her get inside.

Driving along the interstate, Kenya closed her eyes remembering the day she met Storm at the mall and he bought her that designer suit she'd tried on. She thought back on the first time they made love and the day he asked her to marry him. "Do you love me?" Kenya turned her head to face him.

"Yeah, I love you!"

"Say you promise!" She gave him a faint smile.

As they pulled in the driveway, Kenya got a glimpse of London's and O.T.'s silhouettes through the blinds and got sick to her stomach. She made Storm swear that he wouldn't let his brother or her sister say anything to her until she was ready to speak.

"I just wanna go up to my bedroom and go to sleep."

"Don't worry, boo-boo, I ain't gonna let them stress you the fuck out tonight. I got you!"

When they walked through the front door of the condo all eyes were on them. Kenya quickly became the center of attention as Storm whisked her up the stairs.

Sitting on the edge of their bed, Storm took out his cell phone clearing a lot of unnecessary calls off his log of numbers. Momentarily gazing at the bathroom door hoping when Kenya came out she'd tell him what the doctor had told her, he waited and continued passing the time by erasing several irrelevant text messages that he'd received.

Dressed in her robe, she finally emerged and crawled into bed. "I'm about to go to sleep. Can't we just talk in the morning?"

"Naw, baby girl, we can't." Storm had enough of Kenya beating around the bush and wanted answers.

"Look—"

"Naw, you need to tell a guy something!"

"Well, it's like this." Kenya started her confession as the house phone rang. Leaning over, she picked it up hearing the operator on the other end with a collect call from Tangy. Immediately hanging up, she ran her fingers through her hair and tried to fess up once again but was stopped by the annoying sound of the phone.

"Who the fuck is that?" Storm got pissed.

"It's Tangy's ass!" Kenya rolled her eyes. "I'm too tired to deal with her and all them questions about Paris."

"Then just tell her to stop calling!"

Kenya accepted Tangy's call as she pulled the blanket up over her legs. "Hello."

"Hey, Kenya. Why you didn't accept the charges the first time I just called?"

"Because I'm busy."

"Oh yeah, doing what, thinking about me?" Tangy tried flirting.

"Look, Tangy, I'm not trying to be rude, but I'm busy talking to Storm right now so—"

"So what? You don't have time to hear some good news from somebody who's supposed to be your homegirl?"

"Tangy, what in the hell is wrong with you?" Kenya got loud as Storm went into the bathroom to wash his face.

"Damn, Kenya, just tell me how my cousin is doing."

"Not now, Tangy, besides I haven't been there to visit her this week."

"Oh, so you so stuck back up in that cheat-ing-ass man of yours behind, you abandon your best friend just like that!" Tangy yelled frustrated she wasn't getting the attention that she wanted.

"Listen, you burly bitch!" Kenya gladly returned the attitude. "I don't know who in the fuck you think you talking to, but you got me all fucked up! I ain't one of them little weak-ass hoes you kick it with! Now if I wanna talk to my man or whosoever else's then that's my business. I don't owe you jack shit! You's Paris's cousin and nothing fucking more to me!"

"Yo, sweetheart, you and your man ain't about shit. Don't think 'cause I'm locked up I ain't heard about Royce's boy Marco terrorizing y'all's asses!" Tangy laughed. "The whole town know y'all weak out in them streets! I was just calling to tell ya some good shit, but you on a whole other level. And as for Paris, that's my blood! She don't need you!"

"Good I'm glad she don't!" Kenya didn't realize the time allotted for the call had expired and Tangy had been disconnected as she went on screaming into the phone's receiver. "'Cause her crazy-ass is the reason God marked me and I can't ever have any kids of my own! So fuck you and her!"

Slamming the phone down, Kenya grabbed for the small box of tissue in the drawer of the nightstand. Lying back on the pillow, it then dawned on her what extremely personal information she'd just blurted out to Tangy.

Oh damn! No, I didn't just say that to that bitch! It didn't take long to then realize her man Storm was standing right in the doorway in between the bathroom and bedroom.

"Kenya, what did you just say?" Storm felt betrayed that what he definitely overheard her saying she chose to say to a total nobody first, instead of him. "Is that what the doctor said? You can't have any babies?"

Not knowing what to say or what to do, Kenya mouthed the word no and decided to just lie there looking dumbfounded. It was like she was now living a dream or watching television. All she wanted to do was stop stripping and she did that, move away from Detroit and she accomplished that, run a legal business making lots of money and of course Alley Cats solved that. Praying for a good, loyal, or at least halfway decent man was on the top of her list like every other normal bitch in the world. Thankfully Kenya had found that in Storm and now, through no fault of her own, she wouldn't ever be able to give him a baby.

Even when the three or four specialists explained it was some sort of inherited reproductive genetic trait that must have magically skipped her identical twin, Kenya knew it was God's way of paying her back for killing Chocolate Bunny's unborn child. Now knowing what she knew and London being pregnant with Storm's seed, she balled up in the fetal position refusing to discuss anything with him.

Storm didn't press his girl to talk because he knew how hurt she was. It was evident by the expression on her face. The 100 percent truth of the matter was he himself was devastated about the heartbreaking discovery. Hell motherfucking yeah, he was excited about being a father to his and London's baby in a few weeks, but that still didn't mean he didn't look forward to having more children in the near future with Kenya, who would soon be his wife. Not knowing what to say to console her, Storm dropped his head leaving the bedroom.

London

"Hey, Storm!" London stood hopeful at the bottom of the stairs as he came down. "Is my sister okay? What's wrong with her?"

"She'll tell you when she's ready," he said taking his hand and rubbing her stomach as he had done the day before.

As O.T. observed London not resisting his brother touching her, he knew he'd better step up his game before Storm was banging both twins on the regular.

Chapter 17

If It Ain't . . .

Storm

The next morning Storm got up early leaving the condo without even waking up his brother who, for some strange reason, had been acting distant toward him. He had a few important prearranged meetings with the heating and cooling contractor as well as the painter. Arriving on time they all did a detailed walkthrough of the work that was completed at Alley Cats along with an update on finishing the remaining portion of work.

Tying up all the loose ends of his first stop of the day, Storm pulled out the newly paved parking lot on the way to his lawyer's office. Having an appointment at twelve o'clock sharp to pick up his freshly drawn paperwork, he sat in his car calling Brother Rasul's connect as requested,

confirming he'd be on time for the drop-off later
that day.

"Yeah, I know where."

"Seven," was all the caller said.

"I'll be on time," Storm replied as he turned
off his car and went inside the tall office building.

Police

"Listen up. Keep a low profile on the Christian
brothers," Malloy radioed to both his officers on
surveillance duty. "We just got some crazy evidence from a crime scene we over here working
and by the looks of things something might jump
off in the next few days and we wanna be ready."

"Okay," the first one remarked back. "O.T. is
just leaving out the front door, so I'm on him."

"Yeah, Malloy, Storm just left his club and is
now inside of some office building downtown
near police headquarters," the other reported as
he downed a bottled ice water.

"Both of you just be on alert," Malloy advised.

Placing his two-way radio back on the seat
of the unmarked Town Car, Malloy rejoined his
partner, Kendrick, and three homicide detectives who were searching the apartment of a

murder victim: eighteen-year-old Alexander Robinson Jr., known to all his family and friends as Coonee. More than a month and a half late on his rent, the landlord knocked on the door of her young tenant to notify him the bailiff would be there the next day so he needed to vacate her premises or take the risk of his personal belongings being thrown into the streets.

Instead of being able to issue him a warning she found his door ajar and entered the premises to see what if any damages were done to her property. Five minutes of being inside snooping she saw Coonee's feet sticking out from under a pile of dirty clothes and screamed repeatedly causing the next door neighbor to call the police. When the cops got there securing the perimeter, the evidence tech soon arrived. Less than five minutes later he gathered items off the bathroom floor letting them know Marco Meriwether had definitely been staying there.

O.T.

Peeking in on London who was lying in bed reading a book, O.T. asked her if she needed anything before he left. Reminding her that the doctor wanted her to get as much rest as possible in these last weeks before her due date, London promised to take it easy. He could tell she seemed preoccupied with something, but she was acting hush-hush.

O.T. knew the importance of chasing down Marco making him pay for Boz's death and the other ridiculous shit he'd pulled, but decided to put that task on hold while he handled some personal business. Getting in his car starting the engine he blasted the music loudly disrespecting the neighbors as he took off flying down the block. The officer parked at the far end of the street barely had the opportunity to turn around and catch up.

Having direct orders to stay on O.T. by any means necessary the officer would do his best.

First going to the mall, O.T. turned in valet parking, tossing the attendant his keys. After a couple of hours he exited with over $1,000 worth of baby clothes and accessories. Even though money was tight for him, he chose to go in his emergency stash and do something that would win London's heart. Another store followed that trip to the mall, followed by a couple more.

Next, zooming down the highway on the edge of the state line, O.T. dipped into an apartment complex where he grabbed some brochures and a rental application. Looking at his cell phone to see what time it was, he had one last stop to make to ensure his life would stop being as chaotic as it had been. He parked his car in a space labeled VISITORS ONLY as he entered the secluded two-story building to make his peace.

Storm

Strolling out the law office with a manila envelope tucked under his arm, Storm had a huge grin on his face as he got in his car speeding away. Knowing Kenya was probably hungry he stopped at the local deli, buying her a hot corned beef sandwich on onion roll.

Also thinking about London, who was carrying his child, he ordered her the exact same thing figuring they had the same taste. Storm was gonna go home to try kicking it with Kenya and let her know that baby or no baby he was in her corner, rest up a little while, and chill until the designated time for the drop-off. He was in the best mood he'd been in for months because after tonight, he'd be back on top. Royce, his number one competitor, was out the picture, leaving no one to challenge his takeover bid of the Dallas drug game.

Coming in the house and upstairs he stopped by London's room first, tapping on the closed door. Hearing her give him the okay he entered her room.

"Hey, Storm." London was still reading her book.

"Here you go. I got you something to eat on if you get hungry later."

"It smells like corned beef. Is it?" London turned up her lip putting her hands up.

"Yeah, it is." Storm wondered what was wrong when he saw her reaction. "I thought you'd like it."

"I'm allergic to that kind of meat."

"Dang, your sister loves this shit!" He laughed. "Y'all is different as day and night."

"That's what our grandmother used to say before she passed." London got sad.

"Well look over this and see do this make ya ass break out in bumps and hives!" Storm winked handing London the envelope he'd gotten from his lawyer as he shut her door and went to check on Kenya. Seeing that his woman was up and standing out on the balcony looking at the trees in the backyard he took that as a sign that maybe she was ready to talk to him about the tragic news they both learned the night before. "Hey, Kenya. How you feeling, sweetie?"

"Oh, hey." She tightened her robe.

"I stopped by your spot and bought you your favorite."

"Yeah, I can smell it from way over here." She turned stepping back inside the glass door. "Thank you."

"No problem, but before you eat I wanna tell you something." Storm led Kenya to the bed where they both sat down. "Listen, I'm not gonna lie. I knew in my heart that someday we were gonna have kids and there was nothing in the world that would've made me happier than for us to have a beautiful daughter who looked like you or a son who was, well, you know what I mean."

"Well we both know that shit ain't gonna happen."

Storm reached over holding Kenya in his arms. "That's what I wanna tell you." He vowed, "None of that matters to me. The bottom line is that me and you got the rest of our lives to do our thang. We got so many things going on that right now or even a few years from now that we need to straighten out that a baby wouldn't immediately fit into the game plan."

"Okay, that sounds all good and all, but you about to have a baby. So you already made it clear that you were gonna be there for him."

Storm was quiet for a moment. "You right and I am, but from a distance. When this deal is over this evening, with thanks to you for making it happen, and my cash flow gets back to normal, me and you can get married and go on a long vacation. London is a grown-ass woman and will have to stand on her own. Me and you will work out something with her together about joint custody or at least frequent visitation rights. Shit, the white man do this bull all day and make it work!"

"I know but—"

"No buts, Kenya." Storm promised, opening the bag with her sandwich inside, "Me and you ain't about to let nothing come between our love. You already know what it is! Don't you trust me?"

"Yes, I trust you."

"Good, then eat your food because I gotta leave in a few hours." Storm watched her take a bite while he crunched on one of her pickles.

O.T.

Feeling like a fish out of water, O.T. went up to the silver metal desk that was in front of an extra-thick sheet of Plexiglas that separated it from the rear of the building. Waiting for the middle-aged, stern-faced, heavy-set woman to get off the phone, O.T. spoke up.

"Hey how you doing?"

"I'm good. What can I do for you, son?"

"I'm here to see a patient."

"Okay, what's the person's name?" She tapped the computer keyboard.

"Her name is Paris."

"We need a last name, son."

"Oh, sorry my bad. Her name is Paris Yvette Peterson. I don't know the date when she was transferred here."

"She's in our observation ward. Room 251. Are you the person who called earlier for directions?"

"Naw, that wasn't me."

"Oh, all right then." The lady pointed after pushing the button opening the door. "Room 251."

As O.T. entered the room, he saw Paris who was once full of life and loved to talk cash shit sitting in a chair that was pushed to the window. Standing there for a brief second he could tell that she was in some sort of a trance or something.

"Are you family?" A nurse stopped by to change Paris's IV bag from which she had been getting fed half the time.

"Well, I guess," O.T. muttered shocked his ex-girlfriend was looking the way she was and in the bad mental condition that she appeared to be suffering from.

"Whoever you are, just be tolerant with her. You know she doesn't speak. Miss Paris is alert, but doesn't respond to people."

"Oh, okay," was all O.T. could say as he got closer to do what he'd come to do, which was apologize for all the madness he'd taken her through the time that they were a couple. "Hey, Paris, can you hear me?"

Chapter 18

No More Games

At exactly five-forty Storm backed out his driveway and decided to get a full tank of gas. He thought it would be in his best interest to drive around for a little while before meeting with the new connect to ensure that he wasn't being followed by Marco's psychopathic-ass or the damn authorities. Double checking his surroundings as he left the service station, he drove east to west, then west to south, south back to east, and finally east to north. Feeling confident that he wasn't being tailed Storm took off heading for the designated spot not wanting to be a second late.

After Storm left, Kenya started thinking about her situation and was tired of feeling sorry for herself and deliberately secluding herself up in her bedroom like she had done something wrong. Even though she felt that the

tranquil environment of her home was being
invaded by, O.T. and London's backstabbing
presence, Kenya was going to force herself to go
on about her daily routine the best she could,
which today meant washing several full loads
of laundry that had piled up over the past few
weeks.

Staying down in the basement until it was
time to add fabric softener in the machine Kenya
carried the empty basket up the stairs coming
back in the kitchen.

"Hi, Kenya." London startled her sister. "I
thought you were still in your room because I
saw the door shut."

"Ump." Kenya hardly acknowledged her
twin's words or her huge stomach as she opened
the refrigerator taking out a couple of steaks to
cook for her and Storm's dinner.

London was trying her best to bite her tongue
and keep the peace, but she couldn't do it.
"Kenya, listen to me. I know you're mad at me
and can't understand how I feel, but after I was
raped I thought I'd never be able to have a child.
So when this happened, what else could I do?"
London rubbed her belly. "This might be the
only chance I get to have a baby. Besides I love
my son already."

"Look, London!" Kenya planted her hands
firmly on her hips as she started to degrade

her sister. "We both know from day one you always been jealous of me because you were the fucked-up, 'no nigga paying you no attention,' ugly-ass twin, but that's not my fault!"

"Ugly?" London stood back shocked that her twin could be so cruel and decided to give her a strong dose of her own medicine. "If you haven't looked in a mirror lately we still look as identical as we were the day we were born, of course with the small exception of your man's baby growing inside of me!"

"What in the fuck did you say?" Kenya eyes were on the verge of popping out her head.

"You heard me!" London rubbed her stomach and wasn't going to let Kenya get away with trying to humiliate her any longer. "I said your man's baby!"

Pregnant or not that was the straw that broke the camel's back. She couldn't take the bullshit Storm was asking her to deal with anymore. Kenya raised her hand up in the air smacking London across the jaw with every inch of strength she could gather knocking the expectant mother into the side of the stainless steel refrigerator.

"Bitch! You got me all fucked up!" Kenya showed no outward signs of remorse for what she'd just done as she yelled at London who was clutching her stomach seeming to be in excruciating pain. "You lucky I don't kick that fucking kid out ya guts! I let you stay at my damn house and you lie down and give up the pussy like a ho!"

"Kenya, please! Something's wrong," London begged as her sister left the kitchen stomping up the front stairs then slamming her bedroom door shut.

O.T.

Having explained how he felt, O.T. looked at Paris who was still in a zombie zone, spaced the hell out of her rabbit. Not one time in the twenty-five minutes he'd been there in her room had she even wiggled her finger or turned her head. The few times she blinked her eyes they seemed to have been made of glass, like she was a cheap dime store doll.

"Listen, Paris, stuff with us wasn't always bad. We had some hella good times and you was always a trooper with your shit," O.T. continued with his one sided conversation. "I guess I should've just told you what was up with me and Chocolate Bunny instead of letting you just think it was whatever."

With his head down in his hands O.T.'s cell phone rang showing the condo house number on the caller ID. "Yeah, hello."

"Hey it's me," London moaned as the cordless phone beeped signaling it was going dead. "I need you to come home. I think something is wrong with the baby. I'm in so much pain!"

"Sit tight. I'm on my way!" he begged her. "Just relax. I'll be there!"

"Okay, I'll try." She dropped the phone to the kitchen floor as a strong, flowing gush of water poured out from in between her legs. "Oh my God!"

Not even bothering to say good-bye, O.T. ended his first and probably last visit to Paris by bolting out the room and running out to his car. As he sped away from the parking lot he failed to notice that he had extra company. Now instead of just the undercover police following him another car was hot on his trail.

Confusion . . .

"Kenya! Kenya!" London doubled over screaming out to her sister from the bottom of the stairs. "Please help me, please, Kenya!"

*Why don't that stupid wannabe me bitch shut
the hell up with all that fake crying! Ain't shit
wrong with her!*

"Argggh. Kenya, I need you! My water just
broke and I'm having sharp pains all in my sides.
Please come down here, I think it's time!"

*This ho really think I'm playing with her! She
right it is time! Time I threw her no-good-ass
out my fucking house and take back my life that
she trying to steal!* Kenya continued to pace her
bedroom floor as she thought of her next move.

As the labor pains intensified London continued to call out to her sister several more times
still getting no response. "Kenya! Kenya! How
can you do this? We family! This baby is your
nephew! Please help me!" She held on to the wall
as she tried to make it to the couch and lie down
until O.T. got there to take her to the hospital.

Tired of hearing all the noise her twin kept
making, trying to be the center of attention in
once what was her private domain, Kenya flung
the door of her bedroom open and furiously
marched to London's room. *That's it! Bottom
line! I'm about to throw her shit in the street
and let the landscaping crew out in front get
this cheap bullshit for they wives or girlfriends.*

Snatching her sister's belongings out the
closet that were still on the hanger, then taking

her arm clearing everything off the dresser in one motion, including a brass framed picture of the two of them on graduation day, onto the floor, Kenya grabbed the blanket off the bed to wrap all London's property inside of it with the intention of dragging the entire load to the curb. Before completing what she came to do, the irate Kenya spotted an envelope that had Storm's government name on it. "Tony Christian," she read his name loudly. "What the fuck?"

Kenya tapped her foot angrily as she folded back the flap and pulled out a thick set of papers that were obviously from a lawyer. Taking a quick scan of the twisted legal terms that were throughout the document, they were not a deterrent, as Kenya was fast becoming aware of what the papers she was holding in her trembling hands meant. "That motherfucking lying son of a crackhead whore! That nigga ain't shit! No more lies, huh!" she shrieked out as she looked at the date that was next to Storm's signature. "No wonder yesterday he came all up in this bitch acting like shit was all smiles and fucking handshakes! And that backstabbing slut downstairs want me to feel sorry for her! Yeah, right!"

With papers in hand Kenya stomped back into her room to grab her cell phone off the nightstand. In a matter of seconds Storm was on the line.

"Hey, baby," he answered not realizing the mess had hit the fan.

"Fuck you, nigga!" Kenya roared. "How you gonna just keep playing me like I ain't shit?"

"What is you talking about now?" Storm looked at his watch seeing it was nearing seven as he waited to hear what drama Kenya was bringing to the table this time.

"Don't play dumb!" she started in. "You didn't think I was gonna find out about what you did yesterday?"

"What in the hell is you talking about, Kenya? I don't have time for no nonsense right now!"

"Yeah, I know. It's evident you don't have time for me and how I feel! You about to get your pockets the fuck off craps because I thought you loved me and was down for me, but I guess when the shit really floats to the surface, your only interest is looking out for my whining-ass sister and that no-good, hope it's born retarded with one leg and three eyes in the back of his head bastard of yours!"

Storm was pissed off. "Shut your mouth wishing that bad luck on my son! Is you crazy or what?"

"Oh dang! My bad! I guess I should just fall back and keep my mouth shut while you set up a trust fund for that baby and worst of all two different life insurance policies naming London as the beneficiary!"

Storm sat quietly now knowing exactly what in the hell was fueling Kenya's heated rage. "Listen." He tried to finally offer some sort of an excuse, but couldn't justify it. He had told one too many lies and covered up one too many things to offer any kind of an explanation in the way of making things right with him and his girl.

"Me and you is done dealing! After I kick that grimy home wrecker out you can come and get your shit too!"

"Oh, it's like that?" Storm noticed a strange car pulling up on the other side of the abandoned factory warehouse that had to be the connect so he couldn't argue.

"It's just like that!" Kenya cried before flipping her cell closed heading down the hallway to the stairs with the notarized papers in her hands to confront London with her part in the malicious deception. Only making it three small steps down, Kenya was stopped dead in her tracks by the loud booming sounds of a barrage of gunshots that seemed to be as close as her front yard.

O.T.

Running through red lights disobeying every law on the books in pursuit of getting to a distressed London as soon as possible, O.T. pressed the accelerator damn near to the floor of his car. Relentlessly pushing redial on his cell phone in attempts to reach London or at least Kenya, he received nothing but a busy signal. From the drastic tone in London's voice, O.T. realized that this wasn't a false alarm or no fucking practice run. This shit was real and it must be truly time for her to deliver.

He didn't know what had changed him or his selfish way of thinking over the past few months, but whatever it was he knew he had to be there for London and the baby. Driving down the final stretch of road before turning into his brother's semi-gated community O.T. got a glimpse of a car that seemed to be following him, but considering what was going on at the condo he couldn't care less about the ho-ass police stopping him for violating a couple of traffic laws. As far as O.T. was concerned they could provide him and London with a special VIP police escort to the hospital if they wanted to.

Police

"Malloy, do you hear me?" the undercover officer panicked. "Do you copy?"

"Yeah, I copy. Go ahead."

"Hey, Malloy, it seems like you were right. Something is definitely happening out at the Christian residence. The younger brother left from the mental hospital doing a hundred miles an hour and is almost back at his brother's house I think. I don't know what's going on but I might need backup. I think Marco Meriwether is driving a vehicle at least three cars behind me." The officer pulled over at his regular stakeout position awaiting further instructions.

"What?" Malloy fired back. "I didn't hear you correctly. Did you say Marco Meriwether?"

"Yeah, he's got a hood on his head, but I can see a lot of his braids sticking out!" he noticed as the driver sped pass him and was now directly behind O.T. who was turning onto his block.

"That's impossible!" Malloy puzzled, thinking his officer needed some rest from the long shifts he'd been working.

Face 2 Face . . .

Turning onto the block O.T. had to slow his car down to avoid colliding with the massive convoy of Mexican workers, huge trailers, lawn mowers, blowers, and Dumpsters that lined the road. Having no choice but to park several doors down, O.T. jumped out his ride, which was packed with bags containing stuff for the baby, and started jogging over toward the condo.

"Hey, you coward-ass motherfucker!" The hooded driver of the other car swerved up near the curb, getting out with gun in hand.

O.T. froze, shocked that this Negro was so brazen to come to where he laid his head to try to get ignorant and then be ballsy enough to point a gun at him. "Have you lost your fucking mind? I ought to—"

"Ought to what? Shut the fuck up and be a man?"

O.T. laughed. "Come the hell on, what in the fuck do you know about being a man? Matter of fact get the fuck on. I got business to take care of inside and I ain't got time for this mess!"

"You and ya fake-ass brother think y'all can go around ruining people's lives thinking it ain't no consequences to the bullshit, but trust when I tell you it fucking is!"

"Listen, you piece of shit!" O.T. boldly shouted. "If I'm supposed to be scared because you got a gun then you wrong. Now if you gonna do something then pretend you man enough to do it or beat it! But just know I'm gonna hunt ya black-ass down until the day I die for coming out here to my brother's crib!"

"Who in the hell you think you is, Superman?"

"Fuck you with ya bitch-ass!" O.T. spat on the front grass turning around to head for the condo door.

Hearing him making threats acting as if he was untouchable and above getting got, the trigger was pulled and the blazing sound of eight loud gunshots filled the air. Taking cover behind trucks and garbage cans, bystanders witnessed O.T.'s body jerk, absorbing bullet after bullet before hitting the ground.

Chapter 19

One Last Promise

Police

"Malloy! Malloy! Malloy! Send backup!" The officer jumped out his vehicle after witnessing O.T. get gunned down on the pavement of the driveway. "I just saw our suspect Marco Meriwether gun the youngest of the Christian brothers down in cold blood!"

"Don't worry, more than a few squad cars should be there in a few minutes. And don't take any unnecessary risks with whoever the gunman is."

"I told you, it's Marco. I saw his braids!" The confused policeman drew his weapon as the killer's car turned around coming in his direction. "He's getting closer to me as we speak!"

"Naw, guy, you got to be mistaken. Me, Kendrick, and the fugitive apprehension team just snatched a now baldheaded Marco off a Greyhound bus heading east. It seems like he cut off his dreads at the crime scene we were working this morning and then used his victim's identity to purchase a one-way ticket."

"Oh, shit!" The officer tossed the two-way radio on the passenger seat before posting up. Knocking over several garbage cans and hitting a car in an attempt to get away from the homicide that was just committed, the driver was faced with the undercover officer's gun pointed directly at the windshield. "Stop or I'll fucking shoot!"

Not paying attention to the officer's threats the car barreled through the one-man barricade leaving no other recourse, but more gunshots to ensue. Losing control of the automobile after being fatally struck by one of the bullets, the driver crashed into a fire hydrant and slumped over to the side of the passenger seat. As the cocky but nervous policeman approached the vehicle through the heavy water flow spewing from the hydrant with his pistol still drawn, he cautiously opened the door snatching the hood off the driver. As all the braids fell out of the hood, he got a good look at the deceased's face.

"Oh my fucking God!" He frowned, confused as other squad cars finally arrived on the premises followed by an ambulance.

Still wearing a plastic inmate identification bracelet on her wrist, having just been released from jail earlier that morning, Miss Tangelina Marie Gibson, aka Tangy, was pronounced dead on the scene.

Share and Share Alike . . .

Making sure the gunfire had ceased, Kenya poked her head out in total disbelief that this type of madness was happening in her always quiet community. Normally, if there was any type of small disturbance going on it usually involved her and her household. But this chaos seemed to be a couple of houses down. While still holding the paperwork and her cell phone Kenya tip-toed down the staircase listening to all the commotion the people outside were making. Only peeping out the door, Kenya didn't dare go outside not wanting to get involved considering all the illegal firearms they had stashed throughout the condo.

Damn, I wonder what he did. Shockingly she saw the legs of a man face down in the front driveway of her neighbor's house with some of the obviously still rattled landscaping workers gathered around him. Since O.T. had parked several houses farther down the block Kenya couldn't see his car from where she stood and had no way to know that it was Storm's little brother who was badly injured, or, worse than that, dead.

"Help me!" She heard a faint murmured cry coming from the living room. "Please."

Kenya had forgotten about her sister who was the main reason she had started coming down the stairs in the first place. "Is you still perpetrating like you in pain or what? With ya fake-ass! I'm about tired of all this showboating you always doing!"

"Please, Kenya." London reached out her hand to her twin. "Help. I need you."

"Oh, so now you on the floor, huh? What the fuck is wrong with you! You going too far!" Kenya held the papers up. "And what's the deal on this bullshit?"

"Help me, Kenya!" London raised her other arm and that's when her twin noticed a hole the size of a quarter in her upper shoulder blade that was bleeding.

"Damn!" Kenya panicked throwing the papers on the couch looking at the broken window on the far right side of her living room. "A stray bullet must've come through here! Damn white people in this neighborhood ain't no better than us!"

"I'm hurting so bad, Kenya, and I think the baby is about to come. Will you call an ambulance or O.T. back and see what's taking him so long? Arrggh!" she screamed out in agony taking short breaths.

London had to be in shock and delirious not even realizing that she had been shot. "I love my baby. I love my baby," she whispered as she panted desperately trying to catch her breath.

As the blood soaked through her shirt and she kept rambling on about her and Storm's baby, Kenya became strangely agitated and cold. One part of her wanted to do the right thing and immediately get her sister some medical attention, but the other part wouldn't let her do it. *Look at this backstabber*. With a vengeful demeanor she stood indecisively contemplating what move to make next as her twin lay in the middle of her condo's living room floor bleeding to death.

"Why did you have to fuck my man?" Kenya barked out really expecting to get an answer in the middle of everything that was happening. "That shit was foul!"

Hearing ambulance sirens in the distance, London mistakenly thought they were for her and struggled to get off the floor. Staring at the papers on the couch, with callous intentions

Kenya took her foot pushing London back down and holding her there.

"My baby, my baby, my baby," London kept repeating holding her stomach.

Kenya saw her sister's body start to shake and heard her voice get louder. Not wanting anyone to overhear the desperate cries for help, she went over to the CD player turning on some jazz to drown out the noise. Getting down on her knees, Kenya then helped a confused and in pain London take off her track pants and spread her twin's legs wide open. With no medical training to speak of except watching *ER* on television every week for four years straight, Kenya saw that London was right and wasn't pretending. The baby was coming and in fact had already started crowning.

"Where's Storm at?" London sweated tossing her head from side to side. "He said he wanted to be here to see his son born. Is he here?"

"What!" Kenya hissed. "Storm said what?"

"Can you call him for me?" London was in a daze as she kept getting Kenya angrier with her constant pleas for her man as she pushed and pushed. "Storm! Storm! Storm!"

"Shut the fuck up!" Kenya took a deep breath taking one of her socks off stuffing it in London's crying mouth. "Chew on this and stop calling my man! He don't want you to be the mother of his baby! That's my job!"

Five minutes later she was delivering London's baby on the living room floor. Just as the ultrasound had shown months earlier it was indeed a boy. Storm's newborn son had an identical birthmark on his lower backside legitimizing the fact that he was a Christian. Kenya, amazed that she'd successfully delivered the infant, laid the crying baby on London's stomach and went into the kitchen. Opening the drawer near the sink, she searched for and finally found a huge razor-sharp butcher knife with jagged edges. Grabbing a few clean dish towels off the racks and some old bread twists out the junk drawer Kenya spitefully headed back toward a suffering London.

Slipping in and out of consciousness from losing so much blood, London was barely aware of what was going on. Now Kenya, the same person she'd deliberately taunted less than an hour ago, leaned down over her with the knife in her hands lifting the newborn up. Taking the bread twists she wrapped them tightly around the blood-filled umbilical cord and deviously smiled as she thought about Storm. Then vindictively glaring at her reflection in the shiny sides of the butcher knife she cut it off severing all ties the baby had with London.

"Where you going with my baby?" a weak and drained London muttered as the gunshot wound continued to bleed. "Let me hold him. Let me hold my baby," she begged as she started gagging on her own blood.

"Your baby?" Kenya questioned wrapping the crying infant in the dish towels and sat down in Storm's favorite chair rocking him in her arms as she watched her sister struggle to hold on to life. "You must have made a mistake. This is my baby, mine and Storm's!"

"But we're family. We're all we got. I love you, Kenya." London sadly took her last breath.

"Say you promise," Kenya looked down toward the floor and nonchalantly replied ignoring the fact her twin sister had just died in front of her eyes because she chose not to get her any help.

Turning up the music more in an attempt to ignore the sounds of the frantic neighbors knocks who'd recognized O.T. as the gunshot victim, Kenya who had obviously lost her mind hummed to her now deceased twin sister's newborn son while she patiently waited for his daddy Storm to return home so they could be one big, happy family.

"Don't worry, little one, your real mommy's here with you."